Right Place,
Right Time

Second Chances Book Two

By Jennifer L. Allen

Right Place, Right Time

Published: Jennifer L. Allen 2016

jenniferlallenauthor@gmail.com

Editor: Aimee Lukas
Proofreader: Natasha Carrere
Cover Design: Pink Ink Designs

Dedication

To the ladies in my reader group,
Jennifer's Chapter Chicks.
Some of you I've known since the beginning,
others I've only met recently,
but you're always there when I need a hand.
Your ongoing support means the world to me!

Prologue

Kate

Four Years Earlier

"Stupid, no good, piece of crap!" I wince as my sandaled foot comes into contact with the unforgiving tire of my hand-me-down Mercedes convertible. My scowl turns into a frown when I pull my foot back and see the black smudge across the white straps. This day just keeps getting worse!

I tip my head back, look up to the clouds, and pray for a cell signal. When that doesn't work, I bargain. My first born…my soul…good behavior…even better grades…

No such luck.

I'm on a quiet stretch of the interstate, between Columbia and Greenville, where there have been too few passersby, not one of them kind enough to pull over and help the damsel in distress. And, boy, do I look the part of a damsel in distress in a white sundress and sandals with my long, dark blonde hair and big, doe-like brown eyes—the picture of innocence. At least that's what Cedric, my family's butler always says. He nicknamed me Bambi, for crying out loud.

If it weren't for the hot midday sun beating down on my shoulders, I'd probably be terrified. This whole situation has a classic serial killer vibe to it, add in darkness, and I would *not* be standing outside my vehicle right now.

I lean back against the hot car and sigh. What a day. I drove all the way to Greenville to volunteer at an event for a community clinic, just to be informed upon arrival that the event had been rescheduled. They'd posted a notice at the site, which is really helpful when you're one hundred miles away. I frown at my dirty sandal.

Stupid car. Yes, it's a Mercedes, but no, it's not brand new. It's a 1995 model passed down from my father. It has seen many, many better days in its lifetime. My dad has always taken very good care of his cars, hence the reason this fifteen-plus-year-old car is now mine. My parents may be mostly absent from my life, but my dad wouldn't have given me a beater for a car.

Truth is, I probably missed an oil change or something. Whatever. I don't know anything about cars. Ask me to recite all the bones in the human body, and I'll do it. Ask me to name one part of a car, and you'll get crickets. I'm practically a genius, according to my latest IQ score administered by the director of the "gifted program" at my high school, so I'm sure the mechanics of a car wouldn't be too difficult for me to figure out and understand, but this is one of those instances where I'd rather succumb to the gender stereotypes and just play the clueless female role. There's enough information floating around in my brain without my choosing to add more, though part of me kind of wishes I at least knew how to pop my hood right about now.

Hearing the sound of a vehicle approaching behind me, I spin around to look. It's an older sedan, maybe not as old as my hand-me-down, but it doesn't appear to be as well kept. I can just make out that the driver is male through the dirty windshield.

Jeez. I hope he's not a serial killer or something!

I open my car door and busy myself looking for something that could be a potential weapon should this turn into *Wrong Turn.* Empty water bottle, a stack of flyers for another volunteer project I'm working on, a weathered copy of *Gone with the Wind...* I eye the book. It's a hard cover, it might be my best bet.

I hear a throat clear and pop my head up, narrowly missing bumping it on the roof of my car. I can only see his face over the roof of the car as he's standing on the passenger side, lower in the soft shoulder of the highway. My five foot two inch height doesn't help matters either. But wow, if his face is anything to go by, his body must be amazing. He has the most intense gray eyes, almost silver. His nose looks slightly crooked, like it's been broken once or twice, and he has a strong, square jaw with subtle stubble. His hair is buzzed very short so I can't quite tell the color but it looks dirty blond, and he's hot—er—sweaty. Yeah, sweaty. His brow is glistening with it.

He's all man and my seventeen-year-old self doesn't quite know what to do with the attraction I feel. I have *never* felt so nervous around a guy before. *Ever.* I simply don't have time for this sort of thing. Not with my AP classes, studying, extracurricular activities, volunteer work, and college applications.

Smiling wide, I'm suddenly grateful for my vehicular ignorance and damsel in distress appearance. "Hey," I smoothly call out to him, if I do say so myself.

The corner of his mouth lifts in a slight smirk and butterflies take flight in my chest. He doesn't move to come around to my side of the car, which is just fine by me. If he were closer, he'd see the slight trembling of my hands, and he might actually hear the swarm of butterflies.

"Know anything about cars?"

He gives an almost imperceptible nod.

“Do you speak?” I huff, crossing my arms over my chest. What is this guy’s deal? Hot or not, he doesn’t have to be a jerk.

“Pop the hood,” he finally says.

I twist my hands in front of myself and grimace. “I don’t know how,” I say quietly.

He laughs, and I narrow my eyes at him. Whatever. I cross my arms back over my chest and roll my eyes, not appreciating his display and letting him know it.

“There should be a lever just below your steering wheel, feel around for it and pull it out.”

I open my car door and sit down, doing as the hot jerk says, and feeling around for a lever. I find something and pull. There’s a pop, and it looks like the hood might be a little higher than it was a second ago. I grin, pleased with myself.

I catch Hot Jerk watching my little display, and he smirks. I sneer at him, which only turns his smirk into a smile. He has a really nice smile. Hot Jerk walks around to the front of my car and starts wiggling something around in the grill. I get out of the car and approach the front, jumping back as he pulls the hood all the way up.

“Easy there, Sunshine,” he says in a deep, smooth voice I only got a small taste of moments ago. “Don’t want you falling into traffic.”

No, no we don’t.

I have this heady feeling, and I can feel my pulse thrumming through my veins. It's like there's a current running from his body to mine. I realize I'm standing only an inch away from Hot Jerk and take a sudden step back.

"Don't worry, Sunshine. I'm not going to hurt you," he says, sounding resigned.

"I'm sorry," I say, truly feeling sorry but uncertain as to why. "It's just that I'm a single girl, all alone on the side of the road and you're a..." A what, Kate? A stranger? Are you going to go all stranger-danger right now? "I don't know you at all. Can you blame me for being a little freaked out right now?"

"Not at all. And you should be freaked out. You never know what type of people are out there and would stop for a pretty little thing like you."

My cheeks heat up...definitely from the heat, not the compliment. I'm sure the pinkish hue that now stains my cheeks is due to all this time spent in the sun. Yep, that's it. But what an odd thing for him to say...is it a warning? Somehow, I don't think so. I think I'm safe with this guy. I feel it in my bones.

"So you're good at this kind of thing?" I say after a minute, gesturing to the car and trying to change the subject.

He smiles a little; I really like his smile. "Yeah, I've enjoyed tinkering on cars ever since I took auto shop in high school."

I smile back at him and watch as he uses a small flashlight I hadn't realized he'd had to look around the engine. I can't help but notice his furrowed brow and the strong lines of his face as he focuses on the task at hand.

"I think I found the problem. Was there steam coming from under the hood when you stopped?" He asks, standing up straight and facing me.

I nod my head. "Yeah, really freaked me out. I've been out here about an hour already. It stopped after maybe thirty minutes."

He nods. "It overheated."

It and me, both.

"I have a jug of water in my car; let me get it."

I watch him as he walks around to the back of his car and opens the trunk. He returns a moment later with the water and carefully pours it into a small opening near the front of my car.

"This should get you to the next exit," he says. He tops it off, replaces the cap, and lowers the hood, dropping it at the very last minute to allow it to catch. The bang it makes as it drops causes me to jump.

"Thank you," I tell him. "I really appreciate it. I don't know what I would have done if I got stuck out here all day. Or worse…"

"You're welcome," he says with a smile, then begins walking back to his car.

"Wait," I say. *What am I doing?* He stops and turns around slowly. When his silver eyes meet mine, I shiver despite the heat. "What's your name?"

"Jay. Jason Spencer."

Jason Spencer.

"Well, it was nice meeting you, Jason Spencer," I say, stepping forward and sticking out my hand. "I'm Katherine Dumont, but my friends call me Kate."

He takes my hand in his, and I feel it...the electricity.

"It's nice to meet you, too, Sunshine," he beams at me.

By the time he lets go of my hand, I swear I've melted into the ground.

Wow.

Wow.

I can't help but watch him walk away...and hope, wish, and pray that I'll see him again someday.

***

Three days later, I'm sitting in one of my favorite sandwich shops reading. As I snack on a chocolate chip cookie and sip on some sweet tea, a ruckus on the other side of the dining room attracts my attention.

It's a couple of guys around my age horsing around with each other, but that's not what keeps my attention.

It's him.

Jay.

No, it couldn't be. But it is. Jason Spencer is in the same restaurant as me. What are the chances? Do I try to get his attention? Gosh, I want to!

One of his buddies spots me gawking at him and nudges his elbow.

Shit!

Jay turns to see what his friend is pointing at—or who, rather—and narrows his eyes at me for a moment, probably trying to determine if he's hallucinating. Either that or he's already forgotten about me and is wondering why the odd girl is looking at him.

I smile and give him a small wave. My heart nearly beats out of my chest when he returns my smile and starts walking towards me.

"Sunshine," he says in that deep, husky voice of his.

"Jay," I smile, certain that my face has already experienced eight shades of pink since we first made eye contact.

"I didn't realize you were from around here."

"I didn't realize you were from around here, either." *Nice, Kate. Real smooth.*

He laughs. "Right. Well, my friends were just leaving," he gestures to the group of guys making their way out of the shop.

My smile fades away. Just my luck.

"Do you mind if I join you?" he asks, putting his hand on the back of the seat opposite me.

My smile returns as I shake my head. "Not at all, please sit."

***

Jay and I spent four hours chatting in the sandwich shop that afternoon. We even ended up staying for dinner. When he asked me out to dinner and a movie the following night, I accepted without a second thought.

There was just something about him. Something about us. We clicked.

And now, here I sit alone in my parents' large, cavernous house.

Waiting.

He'd said he'd pick me up at six, but it's seven now. He said he didn't have a cell phone, so we never exchanged numbers. I can't even call him to make sure he's okay.

I shake my head at myself. He's gorgeous and older than me by more than three years. I'm just a girl to him. A stupid, naïve girl.

I go up to my room and change out of the little black dress I'd purchased this morning just for our date, kicking it to the floor of my closet and shutting the door. I dress in some comfy pajamas and retreat to my bed, curling up under the covers.

It would be stupid to cry. I don't even know him. I'd just wanted to know him.

I grab the remote off my nightstand and turn on the television. I flip through the channels, hoping to find reruns of *The Nanny* or *Golden Girls*, when an image flashes by.

Wait, what?

I flip back, trying to find it.

There it is.

There *he* is.

Jay.

Chapter One

Kate

"One Black and Tan and one Killian's," I set the two pilsners down on the high-top table with a smile. "Would you like to order any food tonight?"

"None for me," the black haired guy says.

"We'd like to start a tab," the bald one states as his eyes seem to undress me from head to toe. It takes everything I have not to visibly cringe. You don't get good tips by recoiling from your customers.

"I'll take care of that for you. My name is Kate, holler if you need anything." I quickly move away from the table and check on a few others on my way to the back for a bit of reprieve. St. Patrick's Day is always a great day to work because the tips are generally high, but it brings out the creepers, even to an upscale establishment like Five.

I step outside the back door and take a deep breath of fresh air. The salty bay air is mixed with a little exhaust from the highway and a little garbage from the nearby dumpster, but it's close enough to fresh.

"Kate," Laurie, Five's hostess, calls out through the cracked back door. "You have a visitor."

A visitor? I know it's not Casey, or any of my classmates from school, since none of us can afford a place like Five on our starving student budgets. Could it be my parents? That thought makes me laugh out loud, garnering an odd look from one of the dishwashers I pass on my way back through the restaurant. It would be extremely unprofessional for a professor to ask for me at work, so that can't be it...

I continue to wrack my brain of the possibilities as I weave through the crowded bar area and make my way to the hostess stand. Out of the billion scenarios I'd imagined in my head, not one of them included *him.*

I nearly trip over myself coming to an abrupt stop just a few steps away.

He hasn't seen me yet; I can still make a run for it.

Not the most mature thought, I admit. I'm just not sure I can handle this...handle *him.* What is he doing here after all this time? How the heck is he in California? How did he even know where to find me? He'd told me flat out he stopped reading my letters. It's been *years* since I'd last seen or heard from Jay, and during that final visit I'd gotten the impression I'd never, *ever* see him again. I'm not going to lie, it had hurt. Bad. And he knew it. So what is he doing here now? On the opposite side of the country from where he should be.

Before I can decide whether to speak to him or run far, far away, he looks up and sees me. His cold, gray eyes drill into me, taking me in from head to toe in a much more invasive way than the bald guy at my table, yet it makes me tingle with desire rather than unease. I don't move and I don't speak, I stand stock-still as he continues making his assessment, expecting him to turn and flee once he's gotten his fill. I'm sure he's real impressed with my uniform—knee-length pencil skirt and long sleeve button-down shirt, both in black, with a small red scarf tied around my neck. Standard Five uniform.

Jay looks about the same as he did the last time I'd seen him with the exception of his hair. It's a little bit longer than the super short buzz cut, with some messy spikes on top. His hair is dark blond, I note. He's clean shaven and he's got a small scar on his left cheek. A tremor runs through me at the thought of how he might have gotten that. He hadn't had it the last time I saw him. His square jaw is locked in a perpetual scowl he seems to have gained proficiency in over the years.

When his eyes meet mine again, he doesn't flee, instead he hesitantly steps forward and my breath catches. *This is it.* This is the moment I've been waiting years for. The moment when he says, "I'm sorry; I was an idiot." Only he doesn't say that. He doesn't say that at all.

"I shouldn't be here."

Those are the words that come out of his mouth. After *years...that's* what he says to me.

"Then go," I tell him flatly, pure disappointment flowing through my body. Without wasting another moment, I turn away from him and go back to the busy dining room. I will not let him affect me the way he did before. I will *not* give him that.

***

Laurie seated *him* in my section thirty minutes ago, and I haven't been by his table once. I'm pissed he's taking up space, but I know he'll leave a tip whether he orders or not. That's just the type of guy he is. At least I think it is. It's the way he had been when I thought I knew him. I guess it turns out I hadn't really known him at all. But still, there's just something about him...something I've trusted since the moment I first saw him...which is completely crazy, considering his past.

Deep down though, I know he's a good guy. He's a good guy trying to do the right thing. Isn't that always when they hurt us the most? When they think they're doing the right thing? Whatever.

Bald guy is pretty lit and black-haired guy is unsuccessfully trying to get him to chill out. He hasn't made a grab for me yet, but he's been getting closer and closer every time I pass by their table. I've only served him two Black and Tans, so I suspect their evening started before they'd arrived here tonight, either that or he's an incredible lightweight.

While I'm at the bar getting refills for my less obnoxious guests, I chance a look at Jay. He's tucked away at a high-top table in the corner by a window. His feet are resting on the lower bar of the stool, his knees are bent, and his elbows are resting on the table. His head is down, focused on the paper coaster he's decimating with his hands. When he was standing at the hostess stand earlier, he looked like a rugged man in his black work boots, faded jeans, and leather jacket that covered the sleeves of tattoos I know he has. Now, hunched over the table like that, he reminds me of a vulnerable boy.

"Order up," the bartender, Ted, says, and I pick up my tray of drinks. "That table treating you right?" he asks, nodding to bald guy's table.

"So far."

"You let me know if they get out of line."

"Thanks, Ted." I give him a smile and move to deliver the drinks to my table.

Ted's a...nice guy. He's in his early thirties, tall, dark, and handsome with brown eyes and brown hair. He could be a really great friend, too, if he didn't have a crush on me. He's worked at Five as long as I have and asks me out at least once a season. I find a way to politely turn him down every time, with school being the most frequent excuse. I'm pre-med at Stanford, and I truly don't have the time for a relationship or dating. I also never really envisioned a guy almost ten years older than me being my boyfriend. Not that there's anything wrong with dating older people, it's just not for me at this stage in my life.

Still, it's good to have Ted around on nights like tonight when patrons can get a little out of control. He's not overly buff or anything like that, but he practices martial arts, so he's got some moves. It helps considering we don't have bouncers like many of the other bars around. We're known for our upscale cuisine, not as a drinking establishment, but the "rules" pretty much fly out the window on holidays—especially ones celebrated with alcohol.

I deliver my drinks, and as I walk by bald guy, he stops me with a hand on my arm. I gracefully remove myself from his hold and refrain from rolling my eyes as I turn to face him.

"Whatcha doing working at a place like this?" he slurs, and I notice black-haired guy isn't at the table.

He better not have left him here.

"Where's your friend?" I ask.

"You should be working at a place called Ten, not Five." This time I do roll my eyes. It's not the first time I've heard some variation of that line before, and it certainly won't be the last.

"Can I get you some water?" I pick up the empty glasses from the table and set them on my tray.

"I'd like some of this," he says, and before I realize what's happening, he grabs my ass and squeezes.

Stunned, I twist away from his touch. The tray I'm holding crashes to the floor with my choppy movement, and the glasses shatter on the hardwood floor. Nearby patrons shriek in shock and surprise. I'm about to lay into the guy about keeping his hands to himself when I'm gently pushed back and a pair of wide, leather-clad shoulders are suddenly between me and the drunk patron.

"Put your fucking hands on her again, and I'll break them," Jay growls.

This is *so* not good.

"Hey, now, let's calm down here." I peek out from behind Jay to look for the owner of the nervous-sounding voice, and see black-haired guy has returned to the table. *Nice timing, jerk.*

"*Your* friend got handsy with *my* friend. Don't you tell *me* to calm down." Jay's voice is deadly calm, and I can just imagine the look he's giving the two men because black-haired guy's eyes widen as he takes a step back.

"We were just leaving," he mutters. "Can we get our check?" he asks me, not taking his eyes off Jay. Smart man.

"Sure," I tell him, reaching into my apron for the check.

"Everything okay over here?" Ted asks, finally making an appearance.

"It's fine," I hand the guy his check, and Ted says he'll cash him out. I thank him and put my hand on Jay's arm, tugging on it to get him to stop glaring and step away from the dumbass duo. On the third tug, he finally looks down at me, and it's as if he's seeing me for the first time. As if he hadn't even realized where he was until this moment. He looks almost as vulnerable now as he had when he was sitting alone at his table.

"I think you need to go," I tell him. The vulnerability is immediately replaced by a steely resolve as he nods and walks away, stopping by the table to leave some cash before he walks out the front door.

"Who was that?" Laurie asks in awe, walking over and standing beside me as I watch Jay leave.

I shake my head. "I don't know."

And it's true...I'm not sure I know who Jay is anymore. Or if I ever did.

Chapter Two

Jay

"I shouldn't be here."

No truer words had ever been spoken.

So why am I still here?

I pace the parking space beside my restored Harley Roadster, trying to figure out what to do. She'd said I should go. *Twice.* She's probably not going to be thrilled when she walks out and sees that I'm still here. At first, I'd intended to stick around just long enough to make sure those assholes left. But once they were gone, I couldn't bring myself to hop on my bike and drive away. This is the closest I've been in years to the girl I've been dreaming about ever since we first met almost four years ago.

I arrived in California six months ago on a whim. I'd read her letters—all her letters—and had to see her. Truth is...I have no idea what possessed me to physically come here, rather than call or reach out through social media, but I know what's kept me here. And now I've got a month-to-month lease on a cheap apartment near the garage I work at as a motorcycle mechanic. I'm just winging it. Taking it day by day and trying to figure out my place in the world...if I even have a place in the world anymore.

Admittedly, I've seen Kate a few times since getting here, too afraid to make contact. Add stalking to the list of my many stellar qualities. I just didn't know how to approach her...or what to say. I'd said some pretty mean things the last time I saw her and, while I thought I'd been doing it for her own good, in retrospect, it had been a pretty shitty move.

My brooding is put on hold by the sound of laughter. *Her* laughter. I stop pacing and look towards the back exit of the restaurant. Kate, the hostess, and the bartender are all walking out the door. She's looking up at the bartender, laughing at whatever he's saying, and he's looking down at her with stars in his eyes. Can't say I blame him.

I don't know what to make of this guy. He looks like a preppy tool bag, which is exactly the kind of guy Kate should have in her life. Someone safe and smart and stable.

Not a guy like me.

I curse myself for sticking around this long. There aren't enough vehicles in the parking lot for me to duck and cover, so it only takes seconds for the hostess to make me out in the shadows and nudge Kate in the rib with her elbow. Kate scowls at the girl, and the girl gestures towards me. When Kate's brown eyes meet mine, they widen.

Yep, I'm still here!

She says something to her friends and as she walks away from them, towards me, the bartender puts his hand on her arm. She stiffens, and I take a step forward, feeling a possessiveness I shouldn't. I don't deserve to feel anything towards her. She says something over her shoulder that I can't hear, and he lets go, looking properly chastised. I smirk, glad to see she's got some sass. Her friends watch her for a minute, then go to their respective vehicles.

"I told you to go," she says when she steps in front of me.

"I wanted to see you."

"What you did in there wasn't very smart," she continues, ignoring what I'd said. "That situation could have escalated and someone could have called the police."

"Hold on just a minute there, Sunshine. I appreciate your concern for my well-being, but no one is going to treat you that way when I'm around and get away with it. Let them call the cops, I will protect you whenever and however I can. Always."

Her lips forms a surprised "O," and she seems stunned for a minute. Then she shakes her head and comes back to me. "Why are you here, anyway? Not just at the restaurant, but in California? Are you visiting someone or something? Just passing through?"

It hurts a little that she sounds so hopeful my stay is only a temporary one, but that's what I'd wanted, right? For her to not want to be around me? Then why the hell did I come here?

"I kind of live here now," I tell her honestly, rubbing the back of my neck in anticipation of her freak out.

"You what?" she shrieks.

"I moved here in September."

"To Stanford?" There's still a high-pitch tone to her voice.

"San Jose."

"You moved here," she says like she still can't believe it. Hell, I can hardly believe it most days.

"Yes."

"Why? How? Can you even do that?" She furrows her brow and waits for answers.

"I drove here on my bike—"

"From South Carolina?" she almost shrieks again, and I nod. "Are you crazy?"

"People do it all the time." She gives me a look that says she doesn't believe me and she still thinks I'm crazy. Understandable. Even *I* think I'm crazy.

"And you're not going to get in trouble for being here?"

"No, I'm not going to get in trouble," I answer, sounding like a child getting scolded. I feel like a child being scolded, too.

"I just don't get it, Jay. Out of all the places you could have gone…you had to come here."

"I don't get it either," I say quietly, staring at the asphalt under my boots.

"Look, I'm not really sure what you want me to do here," she starts, and I quickly interrupt her.

"Nothing. I don't expect you to do anything. I just wanted to see you. I *needed* to see you."

"That's quite the contrast from the last time we saw each other."

I let out a sigh and lace my hands behind my head, looking up at the sky for a moment as I try to find the strength to explain my fucked up reasoning for doing what I did. For pushing her away. I'd never wanted to hurt her. I still don't. I was only trying to protect her. To keep her safe.

"I was in a really bad place back then," I say after a minute of absolute silence.

"No shit." The way she says it, so matter-of-factly, as she's standing in front of me with her arms crossed, hip cocked, and a take-no-shit attitude has me barking out a laugh. "So this is funny, now?"

"No. I'm sorry," I say, shaking my head between laughs. Then I nod. "Yes. You gotta admit..."

Her lip starts to quirk up on the side. "You have a nice laugh," she says after a minute. "I'd forgotten what it sounds like."

"Thanks. So do you," I tell her. She does. Her laugh sounds like church bells. Holy and innocent. I'd never forgotten that sound. Just one of the things that got me through it all.

She blushes at my compliment and shifts from one foot to the other, finally relaxing her stance. "So you've seen me. Now what?" she asks, briefly lifting her arms to her sides before letting them drop against her hips.

Now I should leave and never look back. Let her live her life, finish school, become a doctor, marry the preppy bartender, buy a house, and have two-point-five kids. And a dog. Can't forget the dog.

Instead I ask, "Want to grab some coffee?"

Chapter Three

Kate

"It's after midnight," *on a school night.* But I don't say that last part out loud because I don't want to sound like a complete dork.

Jay rubs the back of his neck, and I am beginning to realize it's a nervous habit for him. It's that vulnerability again. It's actually kind of nice to see that in a big, tough guy.

"I didn't really think that through. I was just hoping to talk to you some more."

"There's a park near my apartment," I suggest, shrugging my shoulders like I couldn't care less what we do.

"Okay...I'll follow you?" I nod in agreement, eyeing his motorcycle. "I'd offer you a ride," he says, motioning to his bike, "but I only have the one helmet."

I look up and meet his intense stare. "It's okay. The idea of riding on a motorcycle kind of terrifies me. The number of injuries one can sustain from a motorcycle accident is utterly insane. The fact that you made it across the country unscathed is incredible."

"They're not that unsafe," he scoffs, and I narrow my eyes. "It's mostly careless or reckless driving—often on the part of people driving *cars*," he looks at me pointedly, "that leads to those kinds of accidents. And besides, I'm very careful."

"Could be debris in the road," I mumble, still trying to make my point.

He smiles. "You're right, there could be."

I point to my car—the only one left in the lot—and tell him to follow me. He nods and then puts on his helmet, securing the strap beneath his chin. He gets on his bike, then lifts the visor on his helmet and looks at me.

"What?" I ask.

"Are we going?" he asks me, his voice distorted from his helmet, and, even though I can't see his lips, I can tell that he's smiling. He gets these little wrinkles in the corner of his eyes. It's adorable, and kind of sexy. He should smile more often.

Shit. "Yes," I say, hurrying off to my car. *Shit. Shit. Shit.* He totally caught me ogling him! And then I continued to ogle him! *How embarrassing.* I get in my car and quickly start the engine. I pull out of my parking space and move slowly through the lot, allowing Jay to get behind me.

I watch Jay's lone headlight as he follows a safe distance behind me. I can't believe he's here. I can't believe I'm spending time with him. I can't help but remember the last time we saw each other and the hurtful things he'd said.

"What are you doing here?" Jay asks, his cold, silver eyes are like icy daggers, piercing into me.

"Thanks for seeing me," I say with a smile, choosing to ignore his irritation.

"You don't belong here."

"I graduated yesterday. I wish you could have been there."

He scoffs loudly, startling me. "Why?"

I don't want to tell him the truth...that I don't have any friends...that my own parents weren't at my graduation. I don't want him to realize how pathetic I am. How he's my only outlet these days, even though our communication has only been through letters. Until today.

"Would have been nice to see a friendly face," I shrug.

"You think my face is friendly?" he laughs.

He's mocking me. I'm not stupid or naïve. Far from it, in fact. He'd been so nice to me the day we met and the days that followed...I don't know why he's being a jerk now. His eyes were kind that day on the side of the highway. The letters he used to write had been kind, too. He *was kind.*

"I'm moving next week. To California...to Stanford." This information seems to disrupt the cool façade he's displaying. His eyes go soft and his smirk twitches, but only for a moment. I knew he was in there somewhere. I knew this was all an act. He's playing the tough guy...he probably has to around here. See? I'm not stupid.

"Good," he says, cold demeanor back in place. "That means you won't be coming by here again."

"I can still write. Maybe I can call you every once in a while? Or you can call me?"

I jump as he slams his hands down on the table. "Don't you fucking get it? I don't want to hear from you. I don't want to see you. And I sure as hell don't want to talk to you. I don't even read your letters anymore, so stop wasting your time. You're no one to me. Nothing."

My eyes well up with tears just thinking of that day. I thought I'd put it behind me, and I guess I had, but then he showed up again. Out of the clear blue sky. Across the country. Almost as if...as if he'd followed me here.

No. It couldn't be.

He was so adamant that I leave him alone. There's no way he would have come all this way just for me. It's just a coincidence.

You know he had only been trying to push you away...to keep you safe.

I curse the voice in my head for being so logical. So what if he'd followed me here? It's probably just to check on me and that's it. Like an older brother would check on his little sister. That's probably all he sees me as anyway...the little girl stuck on the side of the road...a damsel in distress.

Not the way I look at him. Not that way at all.

Ten minutes later, I pull into the parking lot of my apartment complex and park. He pulls his bike in the space beside me.

"There's no parking across the street," I tell him, looking over at the park.

"Nice car," he says, lifting his chin towards my SUV. "It's new."

"Thanks. It was a gift. I got it when I left for school." My car, a silver 2012 BMW X3, was my high school graduation present from my parents. It's fully loaded with a leather interior and a moon roof, and was delivered straight to my California apartment the summer I'd moved here after high school. The only thing it'd been missing was a bow.

"I bet it doesn't break down on the side of the highway."

I shake my head, holding back a smile at his slight playfulness. "No, I take it in for routine maintenance." I'm much more responsible with this vehicle than I had been with my old Mercedes back in high school. I'm not sure I'll ever be sorry about that, though, since that car is what led me to meet Jay in the first place. "Wanna walk?" I ask, ready to move out from under his intense gaze.

"Lead the way," he says, extending his arm out and bowing slightly.

I giggle at the formal gesture, and we walk side-by-side across the parking lot. When we get to the curb, he takes my hand before looking both ways, then crossing the street. His touch sends a shockwave straight through my system. I look up at him, to see if he feels it, too, but his face is a mask of indifference.

Figures. I feel the earth move, and it's just another day for him. He's probably touched so many women that little ol' me won't make a bit of difference. When we reach the other side of the street, he lets go of my hand.

We sit across from one another at a picnic table in the park, and I shiver, wishing I'd brought a jacket. It was a warm day, but the evening breeze has brought with it quite a chill. Jay sees my dilemma and pulls off his leather jacket, handing it to me over the table. I'm not one to look a gift horse in the mouth, so I eagerly accept it.

“Thank you,” I tell him as I shrug on the oversized coat. “Let me know if you get cold, and I’ll give it back.” He gives me an odd look, as if a man telling a woman he’s cold is not likely to ever happen. Maybe he’s right. I don’t spend a lot of time in the casual company of others, except for my roommate, but she can be as socially awkward as I am, so I don’t think that counts.

“So…pre-med, huh?”

Chapter Four

Jay

"You read them?" she asks, her eyebrows raise in surprise first, then lower as she blushes, probably remembering what some of the letters said.

"Yes."

"You lied to me?" she frowns, obviously remembering that day she came to see me. I was terrible to her that day and have felt guilty about it ever since.

I shook my head. "No, I hadn't read them then. Only the first few I replied to. I read the rest before I left to come here."

Her mouth forms that "O" of surprise again and I really, *really* wish she'd quit doing that.

Every time she draws attention to her lips I just want to kiss her, and that is not something I need to be thinking about. Not now. Probably not ever.

She looks down at the table and rolls an acorn between her delicate fingers. “I'm a different person now than I was when I wrote those letters,” she says solemnly.

“I'm sorry I didn't read them sooner.”

She just shrugs her shoulders. “Not much you could have done for me then.”

“You needed a friend, and I bailed on you.”

She shrugs again. “It was years ago. Things change. If that's the only reason you're here, then you're free to go.” Her tone is no-nonsense, and her glare is glacial as she gets up and walks away.

I watch her walk over to the swings, torn over what I should do. When I first met Kate, she was a burst of sunshine in my otherwise cloudy existence. I'd been living life one day at a time, just trying to get by...trying to survive. Trying to get over my past. Then one day—out of the blue—there she is. All I could think is that I must have done something right in my life for that beautiful creature to have been placed in my path that day.

After everything went south for me, I never thought I'd see or hear from her again...how could I? Then the letters started. I thought seeing her name, Katherine Dumont, on the return address had been a hallucination. I'd wondered how she'd found me—not realizing at the time that she was quite resourceful. I read that first letter, feeling the excitement of an elementary school kid getting letters from a pen pal. I wrote back to the first few, answering her questions and telling her everything about me.

Then shit got tough for me, and I'd stopped. The letters kept coming, but I set them aside. In the end, there were more than fifty letters—all unread.

After nearly two months of living back home with my brother, I'd finally broken down and started reading them again. I'd missed her, and I selfishly wanted her back in my life. I sorted them by postmark and started with where I'd left off. They were chipper, cheerful...just like I remembered her. By about the tenth letter though, her tone had changed. I'm not sure how you can read a tone in a letter, but you can. By letter twenty-five, gone was the optimistic girl I'd dubbed "Sunshine." In her place was a sad and lonely girl. And it only got worse. That's when I knew I had to see her. I had to see with my own two eyes that she was okay.

The decision to go to California was a spur of the moment one and not easy to arrange, but with the help of my brother, Mac, I'd made it here. Trying to find her at Stanford would have been like trying to find a needle in a haystack, so I did some Facebook recon and managed to find out where she worked. After spending three evenings parked in the lot across from her restaurant, I finally saw her.

And she looked...good. She wasn't the bubbly, happy teenager I remembered, but she looked healthy, and I caught a smile as she said goodnight to her co-workers. She looked older—in a good way—and more mature. She looked really good.

I guess in my head I'd conjured up this image of Kate needing me and, for once, I wanted to be the piece that made someone whole again. But it didn't seem like Kate needed my help at all. Still doesn't. From the few words we've exchanged tonight, it seems like she's strong and confident...not the girl from the letters. She'd been right about that.

I watch as she kicks her legs and swings higher and higher, seeing a glimpse of that girl from long ago. I wish her long blonde hair was down so I could watch it blow in the breeze like it did that day on the highway.

Hell, if I really had a wish, I wish I could go back in time and meet Kate months before my life fell apart instead of just days. Long before I made the biggest mistake of my life, one that will follow me around forever. If I had known her sooner, maybe I would have been in a different place that night. Maybe I would have been with her instead of at that gas station.

I get up from the table and walk over to where she's swinging. She slows down as I approach. "I know you probably don't believe me, but I am sorry. I'm sorry I stopped reading the letters, and I'm sorry for the way I spoke to you when you came to see me. You didn't deserve that."

"You're right, I didn't." I let out a sigh. She's not going to make this easy, not that I'd expect her to. "Why tonight?" she asks.

"Hm?"

"Why tonight? You've been here for what? Six months? Why'd you wait until now?"

I take a seat in the swing next to hers and kick at the woodchips below. "I don't have a good answer for that. I got here in September. I...uh...saw you back then."

She turns her head quickly to me. "You've been...what? Following me?"

"Not really." *Kind of.* "I just wanted to make sure you were okay. When I read the letters I freaked out. I needed to see you."

"How did you find me? And how long have you been stalking me?"

Why didn't I think this through? Now I'm coming off as a complete creeper. "I found you through Facebook, and I swear I'm not stalking you. I saw you for the first time back in September, and I've just sort of checked up on you a couple times since. To make sure you were still okay. God, I know this sounds creepy as fuck," I say, running my hands down my face. "I swear I had your best interests at heart." I raise my hands in a sign of surrender, hoping she won't scream or call the cops on me.

"I should probably run for the hills, knowing your history." *Ouch.* "At the very least call the cops." I sigh and look back down at the mulch, nodding my head. She absolutely should do those things. "But I believe you." I look back up at her, and she has a small smile on her face.

"You're putting a lot of faith into someone you barely know."

"And you're not helping your case," she says with a frown, stopping her swing.

"Right," I smile shyly.

"So what made you take the leap tonight and finally make contact? Stalkers usually have catalysts for that type of thing, don't they? Is it an anniversary I don't know about?" she teases.

I glare at her, and she laughs. "I wouldn't know about the characteristics of stalkers, but I'm slightly alarmed that you do."

"*Criminal Minds*."

Television. Of course. "And no, there's no anniversary. I just wanted to see you. I couldn't keep doing drive-bys like a creep. I needed to just man up and speak to you. And apologize for being a dick the last time you saw me. For not writing..."

"You really hurt my feelings back then," she says quietly. "I just wanted to be your friend."

"I know, and I'm sorry," I sigh. "I just didn't want you hanging around that place and waiting on me for...whatever. I don't know.

You just deserved a lot better than a friend like me."

"How about you let me be the judge of my friends?" she asks.

"Deal."

"So, as you said, we don't really know each other...at least not anymore," she says, kicking off again on her swing.

"Well, I think I know you pretty well now," I kick off, too. I haven't been on a swing in years. It feels good...freeing almost. I feel kind of like a kid again.

"Not that girl anymore, Jay," she reminds me in a firm tone.

I smile, liking the sound of my name rolling off her tongue. "You mentioned that."

"So what do you say we start from the beginning?"

"Planning on breaking your fancy new car?"

"Ha ha. Very funny, Mr. Spencer." She blushes when I wink at her. "Not that beginning."

"You want to be pen pals again?"

"No," she draws the word out like she's talking to a child. To someone with her IQ, she probably feels like she's talking to one. "How about you meet me for lunch on Saturday?"

My memory flashes back to the lunch we shared years ago, when we spend hours getting to know each other. It would be nice to have the opportunity to do that again. "I'd like that, and I'm off that day."

"Me, too," she smiles. "There's a café around the corner. We could meet there? Or you can come here, and we can walk together?"

"Let's meet here," I nod in agreement. Meeting her here and walking together means we'll get to spend more time together.

She stops her swing and stands up. "Well, Jay. It's been fun, but I have a nine o'clock class tomorrow so I need to get some sleep."

I rise from my swing, and we silently return to the parking lot. I take her hand again when we're crossing the street, and just like the first time, a current runs straight through her hand to mine. I glance over to see if she's noticed, but she's looking away. This time, I don't let go of her hand when we reach the other side; I don't let go until we reach my bike, which she eyes with disdain.

"Don't be a hater," I tell her, giving her a nudge with my elbow.

She rolls her eyes. "We should exchange numbers...in case something comes up on Saturday."

"Right," I nod, rattling off my phone number. Her lip quirks up on one side when I give her the familiar area code. She types my number in her phone, and a moment later, mine buzzes in my pocket. I pull it out and see a text from the same area code. I program her number in my phone as "Sunshine."

"I'll see you Saturday at noon," she tells me.

I look up at her russet colored eyes and smile. "It's a date. I mean..." *Shit, I give up.* Sighing, I say, "Yeah, I'll see you then."

She laughs and leans in to give me an awkward hug. Well, her part isn't awkward, but mine is. I don't know what to do with my hands. I want to touch her, but I don't feel like I should. I end up awkwardly patting her on the back. Why the *hell* can't I just be normal around this girl?

"It was good to see you," she says, backing away from me with a shy smile on her face. "Good night, Jay."

"Good night, Kate." I watch her walk up the stairs and wait until I see her disappear into her apartment before starting my bike and riding away.

I guess that could have gone worse...

Chapter Five

Kate

I quietly shut the front door and lean back against it, smiling to myself. What an unexpected turn of events. I shake my head when I hear Jay's bike start up and roar off into the distance. Death trap.

"You're home late," my roommate, Casey, calls from the kitchen, startling me. "And why do you look all flushed?"

"What are you doing up?" I ask her, ignoring her questions. I kick off my non-skid shoes, making a mental note that I'll have to clean them before my next shift since the dirt and dust from the park is stuck to whatever restaurant gunk had already coated them.

"Couldn't sleep," she says with a shrug, staring into her tea cup as if it holds the answers to the universe.

"You feeling okay?" I ask, resting the back of my hand over her forehead as I walk by.

She wiggles away from my touch. "Yes, mom." I laugh at her as I grab a cup and fill it with the Brita pitcher from the fridge. I sit at the table and take in the tired, brown eyes of my friend.

Casey and I have been roommates since freshman year; we got on like a house on fire. I thought I'd won the dorm lottery when I got matched with Case, though she would argue that it was her who'd won. We've faced some obstacles over the years with her health issues, but in the end, we've come out stronger. We're all each other has out here. As much as she drives me crazy, she's my best friend. My only true friend, really.

Maybe that's about to change, though. Maybe Jay will end up being my friend, too.

"You've got that look in your eyes again," Casey says, waving her hand in front of my face.

I snap to attention. "What look?"

"That faraway look you had when you walked in. You didn't tell me why you're so late," she points out, raising her eyebrows.

I look at the clock, it's only half past one. It's not like I'm *that* late. But, Casey has a valid concern. Typically, you can set your clock by me. I stick to my routines. I'm predictable. I'm *boring*. Gah, what is Jay ever going to see in a person like me?

"Just a long night at work," I quickly tell her so she won't accuse me of zoning out again. "St. Patrick's Day and all." None of that's a lie, really. It had been a long night at work, at least it felt like it.

She nods, but eyes me strangely, like she knows I'm hiding something.

"So what have you been up to lately? I feel like I haven't seen you at all," I say, changing the subject.

"Studying for exams." Casey is in the psychology program at Stanford. She's as smart as me, if not smarter. We often challenge each other to battles of wits. I know, I know...we're pretty badass.

I groan. "This round has been a beast."

"Tell me about it. I'm looking forward to sleeping in tomorrow."

"I have a test in my nine o'clock."

"O. Chem?"

"Yep."

"And you worked tonight? Are you crazy?"

I shrug. "I was originally scheduled to be off, but someone had an emergency."

"I'm pretty sure an exam in Organic Chemistry is a bigger emergency," Casey tells me. Her raised eyebrows and the death grip she has on her mug demonstrates just how freaked out she is on my behalf.

"Relax, Case. I got this," I say, reaching across the table and patting the hand gripping the mug until she loosens up. Sure, I'm not going to be in ideal form tomorrow morning, but one of the many benefits of having an almost eidetic memory is that I don't have to be in ideal form. "But I *am* going to head to bed. I'm exhausted."

"Don't forget to set your alarm," she reminds me as I get up from the table and place my glass in the sink.

"I won't, mom," I tease her.

We're both laughing as we say goodnight, but she stays at the table, staring into her tea, while I head off to my bedroom. I wonder what that's all about, but I don't dare pry. Casey will tell me when she's good and ready, just like she knows I'll tell her what's up when I'm good and ready.

***

As I'd suspected, I aced my O. Chem. exam. The exam was electronic, so it was graded instantly. We're able to log right into our accounts after the exam and see our results. Mine's a ninety-eight. Not a perfect score, but it will do.

I'm heading across campus to my car when I hear the hum of a motorcycle engine. My heart speeds up as I look around, trying to locate the bike. Then I realize what I'm doing and roll my eyes. Jay is *not* the only person in California with a motorcycle.

As I'm walking, enjoying the warm spring air, my cell phone starts ringing the *Jaws* theme music. The ringtone I have set for my *mother.* Why is she calling me?

"Hello, Mother," I answer.

"Katherine," she replies in her take-no-prisoners attorney tone. It's her only tone, really. "How was your exam?" *Of course.* She has copies of all my syllabi. She knows when I have exams, when I should be studying, when I should be in class. *When I'm on break...*not that *that* matters.

"I got a ninety-eight," I tell her, proud of myself.

"Did you not study?" she asks, her voice stained with disgust. I can picture her cold stare and curled lip.

"Yes, I studied, Mother."

"I expect you to do better next time. Does this professor offer extra credit? You know how I feel about extra credit, but if you can make up those points..." she keeps talking, but I stop paying attention. I've reached my car, but instead of getting inside—where I'd be able to hear my mother in surround sound thanks to Bluetooth—I lean against the side and watch the other students ambling about.

They're smiling and laughing, talking with their friends. They're all probably elated to have finished their exams and passed. Maybe some of the ones on cell phones are talking to their parents, and instead of berating them for not achieving a perfect score, their parents are praising them for having passed at all. I allow myself one moment, just one, to imagine what it might be like if I were one of them.

Normal.

Regular.

Average.

"Katherine! Are you listening to me?"

"I'm sorry, Mother."

"Did you hear what I said?" she asks, plainly seeking an opportunity to call me out on yet another mistake.

"No. I'm sorry, Mother." I don't try to make an excuse. None would be acceptable.

Adelaide Dumont expects the very best from her only daughter. Nothing below perfection is allowed. Perfect grades. Perfect health. Perfect looks. Once, when I was in the third grade, I'd gotten sick. She'd insisted that I continue to go to school until I eventually ended up hospitalized with pneumonia. Even then, she'd had a school-approved tutor at my bedside, breathing mask and all, every day until I returned to school—just so I would still have perfect attendance. The tutor pitied me. Instead of working on math problems, she'd read me stories from some of her favorite children's books. Mother never let me read children's books. Janine Darcy was the tutor's name. I never saw her again, but I'll never forget her either.

"I said your father and I will be spending two weeks in Los Angeles. We'll expect to see you for dinner one night."

Two weeks and they only expect to see me one night. Anyone else see what's wrong with this picture? I mean, I get it. Really, I do. My parents never wanted kids. They'd admitted that much to me years ago. They had me to keep up appearances and pass on their legacy. Maybe they would have liked me better if I was a boy. I was raised by nannies and spent more time with the help than I did with my parents. I've never known them as "Mom" and "Dad" like my classmates knew their parents. They were always "Mother" and "Father." While some children's first words were "Mama" or "Dada," mine was "Baba"—an attempt at saying my nanny's name, Bonnie. Those things considered, why would they want to spend time with me? It's nothing new for me; I'd gotten used to it long ago. Doesn't mean it doesn't sting every once in a while.

"Of course, Mother. Just let me know the date, and I will make myself available."

She lets out a derisive laugh. "Make yourself available...as if you're even busy. You're a student, It's not like you have a *real* job." I don't say anything because, really, what is there to say? Nothing that won't get me chastised or mocked. "I'll be in touch. Don't forget the extra credit," she says just before I hear the click of her disconnecting the phone.

I drop my cell back in my bag and take a deep, cleansing breath. Peeking into my backseat, I see that I have my gym bag. Perfect. I unlock the car, hop in, and start the engine. Careful not to run over any of my happy classmates, I back out of my parking space and head over toward Sand Hill Road. I'm thinking a kickboxing class, followed by some yoga, is just what the future doctor ordered.

Chapter Six

Jay

In the bright light of day, it's easy to see what appeals to Kate about this neighborhood. I arrived early for our lunch date, a little too early. I've been sitting in the park across the road for the past twenty minutes, taking in the scenery and people watching. There seems to mostly be a mix of college students and young, working professionals in her complex. I've also seen a handful of people walking dogs, one couple with a stroller, and an elderly woman being escorted from one of the first floor apartments to a waiting van with the local senior center logo on the side.

The most obvious characteristic is that it's rich. Aside from maybe ten cars in the parking lot, they're all expensive sports cars, luxury vehicles, high-end sedans and classy SUVs—Kate's car included. One of the many reminders that this girl is completely out of my league. I know from her letters that her mother is a lawyer and her father is some kind of doctor—a plastic surgeon maybe? So it's obvious she comes from money. Hell, even the car that broke down years ago had been a Mercedes.

I'm sitting at the same picnic table we sat at last night, only I'm backwards on the bench and leaning back against the table. I have a straight view to her apartment from here, so I'll be able to see when she comes out. This spot seemed like a better place to wait than in direct sunlight in the parking lot. I wasn't sure if she'd want me to knock on her door. A guy who looks like me—biker boots, worn jeans, plain t-shirt, and sleeves of tattoos—in a place like this? Someone might call the cops.

About ten minutes before noon, her apartment door opens, and I stand up, ready to meet her. But it isn't her who comes out, it's a girl with brown hair. She looks to be the same age as Kate, though. I sit back down and watch as the girl walks down the stairs and gets into an older model Honda, then drives away. Must be her roommate.

A few minutes later, the door opens again and this time Kate exits. I stand, and, instead of running across the street like a fool the way I want to, I take her in. Her long, blonde hair is loose, hanging down her back in curls—just like it had been the first time I saw her. She's wearing a yellow dress. She really is like sunshine. I make my way across the street—surprised I don't get hit by a car since I definitely don't look both ways before crossing—and walk up to meet her on the sidewalk.

"Hey," she gives me a beautiful smile.

"Hi," I say as I step up beside her.

"I didn't hear your bike," she says, looking around the lot.

I point to the shady corner of the lot. "I got here early, I've been sitting in the park."

"Oh," she frowns. "You should have come up."

I look away from her, not wanting her to see my shame. "I didn't know if you'd want me to."

"Why the heck wouldn't I? I invited you here."

I look back to her and smile. She's got a heart of gold. The sweetest person I've ever met. "Shall we?" I ask.

"We shall," she says with a laugh.

"So where're we going?" I ask as we start walking.

"Right around the corner. It's this little café that has the best salads and wraps." Rabbit food. Super. Her steps falter. "I'm sorry, I should have asked if that was okay with you. It's just one of my most favorite places to eat and I assumed..."

"It's okay. I'm a guy. I'll eat just about anything." I smile to reassure her and hope she lets it go. No, I'm not excited to be eating at a place that has the best salads and wraps, but *she's* excited and that's good enough for me.

"I'm so sorry," she says again, looking down at the pavement with a frown.

I touch her arm, and she looks up at me. "It's okay. Really."

She gives me a small smile and nods. "Okay. But you get to pick the place next time."

Next time...so she plans to go out with me again. I think I can get on board with that.

***

I'm pleasantly surprised that the rabbit food café serves more than just salads and wraps. Granted, it's more "clean" eating menu items—whatever that means—but at least I can order a burger. When it arrives, it seems to have more vegetables on it than Kate's salad. She giggles at my grimace, and I love the sound. They can serve me a salad burger every day if I get to hear that laugh along with it.

"So, how have you been? What have you been up to?" she asks in between bites.

“I’ve been…good. Things are different, you know?”

“That’s probably to be expected, though, right? Things change. Three years *is* a long time to be away from home.”

One of the things I like about Kate is that she doesn’t mince words. She’s a straight shooter, through and through. I got a glimpse of that in the short time we spent together years ago…how she says what’s on her mind. And I picked up on that in her letters, too. She speaks so freely. It’s nice after being at home with the people I used to know tiptoeing around me. That shit gets old. Fast.

“Yeah,” I nod.

“So you’re living in San Jose?” she takes a sip of her organic iced tea. This place is unlike any place I’ve ever been.

“Just outside. Near Santa Clara.” I hope she doesn’t ask to see my place because I will *never* bring here there. Someone as beautiful and innocent as Kate does not belong in my neighborhood.

“Where are you working?”

“A garage. A motorcycle repair shop.”

“Do you like it?” she asks, tilting her head to the side. I smile, pleased at her genuine interest in my happiness. Aside from my brother, Mac, and my best friend, Sean, there’s no one else who cares about me—or my happiness.

"It's really great," I tell her after swallowing the last bite of my burger. "I know a lot about car mechanics, but not a lot about motorcycles. I learned a little bit on my way out here, though. And the guy who owns the shop—Leroy—he's been teaching me a lot, too."

She smiles, and her eyes sparkle. "That's really awesome. I'm so happy for you, Jay."

"Thanks," I say quietly as I choke down another swallow of the organic root beer Kate thought I'd like. I don't have the heart to tell her it tastes like shit.

"So what *really* brought you to California?"

I sigh and push away my now empty plate. I can't exactly tell her it was *her* that brought me here. Can I? I'm sure she knows it, though, she's not stupid. Plus, I already told her I'd read her letters and had to make sure she was okay. Why else would I pick up and move to the other side of the country? I don't know anyone else here. I don't *want* to tell her, but I can't lie to her either. Not when she's been so incredibly honest with me over the years.

I finally look up and meet her chocolate eyes. This is it. This is *the* moment.

"You."

Chapter Seven

Kate

Hearing him say *I'm* the reason he came to California makes my pulse race. I feel like I'm on top of the world. Jay Spencer—possibly the hottest guy I've ever seen in my life—came to California because of me. Because *I'm* in California. I pretty much figured that out on my own, but it's nice to hear him confirm it. I can't help but smile like I've just won the lottery. Jay looked a little wary when he'd answered my question, but now he's smiling back at me. And he looks relieved.

"I can't say I'm not happy to hear that, but..." I frown, do I want to go there? We're having a good time, chatting like the old friends we really aren't...do I want to spoil it with talk about the past?

He reaches across the table and puts his hand over mine. “Talk to me.”

I cherish the warmth of his hand on mine. My body hums at the contact, and I hope he doesn’t let go. “What made you think coming here was a good idea? What if I’d hated you? I mean you moved across the country, Jay. If you wanted to check on me, you could have called. It’s just…the way we left things…it wasn’t good. You were mean. Like really, really mean.”

He lets go of my hand and leans back in his seat. “I can’t tell you how sorry I am about that.”

“You already told me you were sorry.”

He nods solemnly; I can see the guilt all over his face. He really wears his emotions on the outside. Jay is a beautiful man, but the years have not been kind to him. The stress and exhaustion are apparent in the dark circles under his eyes and his tight expressions. He needs to loosen up.

“I didn’t know how else to get you to stay away. It was a shitty move.”

“If you’d just asked me to not visit…” I trail off, peeling at the label on my bottle.

“I wasn’t exactly making the best decisions back then.”

I look up at him and tap the table to get his attention. He stops looking out the window and looks at me. “You didn’t do anything wrong.”

"You've got a lot of faith in me," he says dryly.

"You've given me no reason not to have faith in you."

He laughs and shakes his head, a sexy smile spreading across his face. "You're really something, you know that?"

"So I've been told," I wink at him as I stand up to throw out my trash.

He jumps to his feet. "I got that," he says, gathering all our trash and taking it to the receptacle across the room. As I watch him walk across the room in his plain white t-shirt and dark blue jeans, I notice I'm not the only one who has their attention on him. A few other diners are watching him, too. Only rather than looking like they want to undress him, these people are looking at him like he's an outcast. Like he doesn't belong. Is it his tattoos? He's got full sleeves on each arm, I can see how they might draw attention.

I smile as he makes his way back to me, keeping a wide distance between himself and the other patrons. Is this what it's like for him? Do people take one look at him and decide he's no good? Just because he doesn't look like an Abercrombie model? The way he keeps his distance and fixes his eyes on me gives me the impression that this isn't the first time he's been looked at like that.

"Is it always like that?" I ask him when we step outside.

"Like what?"

"People looking at you like..." I can't finish the sentence.

"Like I'm a criminal? Like I'm bad news? Scum on the bottom of their shoes?" He quirks his brow, and I nod. "Goes with the territory," he shrugs.

"That's such bullshit," I tell him, my pace quickening with my fury. I'm getting really angry, and I'm almost as angry at him for being so blasé about it as I am at those people for being so ignorant. "They don't even know you."

"Kate, it's not a big deal."

"It is a big deal!" I yell.

He stops walking and faces me, putting his hands on my shoulders. I look up into his silver eyes. "People see tattoos and cheap clothes and they look at me different. It's only a big deal if I let it be one."

I let out a huff and roll my eyes. "Whatever happened to treating people as equals?" I ask.

He laughs at me. "Yeah...I don't think that's been a thing for a while, Kate."

"So you don't care that people treat you differently because of your appearance?"

"Kate...the kind of people who judge someone by what's on the outside aren't the kind of people I care to be around. So no, I don't care that they treat me differently because I don't care about them. I look the way I want to look, the way I like, anyone who has a problem with that can just get over themselves."

Well, when he puts it that way...

"I appreciate that you're all set and ready to defend my honor, but there are better things you could use your energy on."

My breath catches as my mind immediately goes to a naughty place. Yes...there are better things I can use my energy on. Him being one of them. "Like what?" I ask, looking up into his eyes, which appear heated for just a moment...such a brief moment that I'm not even sure I saw it clearly.

He drops his hands from my shoulders and nudges me to start walking again. "Like finishing school." Dammit. Soooo not where I was hoping he'd go with that. "You really want to be a doctor?"

We walk across the street to the park, him holding my hand as we cross as per usual. I go straight for the swings, needing to feel free as a bird to have this conversation. Instead of having to pump my legs to get some height, Jay steps behind me and pushes.

"In junior high, I was given two options. I call them 'The Dumont Paths to Success, Tracks One and Two.' Track One: med school. Track Two: law school. My parents both suck," I say, surprising myself. While I've thought that for quite some time, I've never voiced it out loud before, and certainly not in front of someone else. I've been trained to keep up appearances and never let my guard down.

"Sounds like it. You didn't have a choice in the matter?"

"Sure I did. I got to pick whether I wanted to be a doctor or a lawyer," I tell him dryly. "Anyway...my parents both suck, but my dad is a little softer than my mom. So I picked med school, because I didn't want to turn out like her." Cold and uncaring, I think but don't dare say. "Maybe I should have gone to law school. Maybe having a protégé would have softened her up." Maybe she would have felt something towards me other than indifference.

"Do you like it?" he asks, repeating my earlier question to him.

"I'm good at it," I answer, shrugging as best I can while holding onto the swing.

"You're brilliant, I'm sure you'd be good at anything you put your mind to. I asked if you like it. Does it make you happy?"

My shoulders slump, and I lean my head against the chain. He slows the swing down and pulls me to a stop.

"Hey...I'm sorry, I didn't mean to pry."

"You're not prying," I tell him, staring down at my sandal covered feet. They're filthy from the dirt and dust in the park. "You asked me a simple question. Do I like what I study?"

"Do you?"

I let out a sigh and shrug. I focus all of that energy he was talking about earlier on not tearing up. No one has ever really asked me how I feel about it all, or what I want. The guidance counselors in high school had admired my drive and ambition and just assumed I was on the path I wanted to be on.

"I like the idea of being a healer, and I know it's something I'd be good at. I know I'll have a career where I'll be saving lives, and I think that will be fulfilling."

"But...," he says, interrupting my practiced response.

"But what?"

"Where's your passion? When you figure out the one thing you want to do for the rest of your life, you've got to feel passionate about it. You sound like you could take it or leave it."

"Teaching," I whisper.

"What?"

"I love to teach. I tutored in high school...it was my most favorite thing to do."

"So why not teach?"

I shake my head. He doesn't get it. No one does. "My parents would never allow that."

"Why are you letting them dictate your future?" he says, irritation in his voice.

"Because they're paying for it," I snap at him.

"Kate...can't you get loans or something? Don't you want to do what you're passionate about? This is the rest of your life we're talking about. Do you really want to be doing something you just feel 'okay' about for the rest of your life?"

"You don't understand," I say, standing up from the swing and stepping around him.

"Then make me," he demands.

I turn to face him. "I told my parents I was interested in teaching, and they made me quit tutoring. Said it was giving me the wrong ideas."

"So do it without them."

"I can't. They'd completely disown me, Jay. I know that sounds petty because I'm an adult, and I already live on the other side of the country, but they foot the bill on my entire life. And they'd pull it all out from under me if I didn't do what they wanted. My apartment, my car, my tuition...everything."

"Okay," he says, putting his arms around me and pulling me into his chest as a few tears break free. "It's okay. Never mind all that." I take a deep breath and breathe him in. He smells like leather and fresh air and maybe a little grease. Nothing at all like some of the other boys I've dated over the years. They'd smelled like the fragrance counter at Dillard's.

Chapter Eight

Jay

I really wish I could get my hands on Kate's parents and just shake the hell out of them. They've got an amazing daughter, and somehow they don't think it's enough...that she's enough. What kind of parents would discourage their child from following their passion? Especially when her passion would lead her to a respectable career? There's nothing wrong with teaching. Nothing at all.

Her letters are starting to make sense to me now. I remember the one where she mentioned that she'd stopped tutoring. That's when her light seemed to have burnt out. When the tone of her messages turned sad. The one thing she had been passionate about was taken away from her. Could they not see it? If I can tell by a letter, surely they could tell just by looking at her.

"I'm sorry," she whispers against my chest.

"You have nothing to be sorry about," I tell her, kissing the top of her head without even realizing I'm doing it. Her parents are the ones who should be sorry.

She sniffles as she pulls away. "I guess this isn't exactly how you wanted to spend your Saturday."

"I just wanted to see you," I tell her, and it's the honest truth. I like talking to her and seeing with my own two eyes that she's okay.

She smiles at that. "Want to head over to my place? We can sit and watch some TV or something. Talk? Or we can stay here," she gestures over to the table where we'd sat and talked last night.

"It feels really nice out here, why don't we hang out outside for a while? I've spent so much time indoors the last few years, I love being out in the fresh air."

She nods, and I follow her over to the picnic table. Once seated, she folds her hands on the table and looks at me. "How's your brother?"

In my letters I'd told her about my family or lack thereof. "Mac's good. He just made lieutenant."

"That's great," she says, smiling brightly. "Is he still with the same department?"

"Yep, Richland County." My brother being a cop has come between us once or twice, but I'm proud of him. He works hard and risks his life every day.

"I bet he misses you. Do you still talk to him?"

"Probably not as often as I should."

"Are things okay between you two?" I had confided in Kate about the blow up between Mac and me; the one that resulted in our not speaking for more than a year. She's actually the one who encouraged me—or told me rather—to get over myself.

"Things between us are good. He actually helped me get over here."

Her eyes light up. "Really?"

"Yeah."

"That's great, Jay," she says, putting her hand over mine and squeezing. It is great. My brother is the only family I've got and as much as we butt heads, I know he truly has my back and is concerned about my best interests. "What about Sean?"

I smile, surprised she remembered my best friend's name. Then again, she has the memory of an elephant, so I shouldn't be surprised at all. "He's good. He's probably going to come out here this summer for a week or so."

"That'll be fun. Does he have a motorcycle, too?"

"Yeah. He's got an Indian."

She narrows her eyes. "I don't know what that means."

"It's a type of bike. A brand name, like Harley."

She nods absently. "Yeah…okay."

"That's it," I say, standing up. "I'll be right back."

She quickly stands and hurries after me. "Where are you going?"

"I'm going to get a helmet, then I'm coming back here, and I'm taking you for a ride."

She stops short and crosses her arms over her chest. "Nuh-uh. No, you're not," she says, standing her ground and shaking her head. She's adorable.

I stop walking and turn to face her. "Just a short ride around the block. I'll go slow. I promise." She starts shaking her head again. "Please," I beg, holding my hands up in front of me like I'm praying. Next I'll break out the pout, and I really hope it doesn't have to come to that.

She wearily eyes my bike in the lot across the street.

"I'll keep you safe. I promise."

She looks up at me and something passes between us. I'm not sure what it is, but I want to find out. I know I should keep this girl as far away from me as I can, but I just can't stay away. I'm drawn to her. The same way I think she's drawn to me. I should tell myself to get on my bike, start riding, and don't come back.

Starting something with Kate can only lead to trouble.

And that trouble is me.

***

I take the turns very slow, but Kate's a natural. She's glued to my back and probably cutting off the circulation in my abdomen, but she leans in on the turns and doesn't make any jerky movements. She's a great passenger, considering she was terrified to get on the bike. Once, on a straight stretch of road, I felt her relax a little and even lift her head from my back. Then we'd approached a bend, and she immediately latched back on.

I pull back into the parking lot of her complex and park, holding the bike steady so she can climb off.

"That was so much fun!" Kate squeals as she hops off, taking off the helmet.

"See? I told you."

"I never said it wouldn't be fun. I only said it was dangerous," she points out.

She has a point. "Well I'm glad you liked it."

"I did!" She jumps up and wraps her arms around my neck, giving me a hug. "Thank you for making me try it." When the front of her body presses against mine, I freeze. Our eyes catch as she slides down my body and, again, that same something from earlier passes between us. My hands move from her back to her waist and stay there. I can't seem to let go of her.

This time, I'm certain she feels it, too. I can see it in her eyes. I can feel it in the way her arms grip my biceps and her body remains pressed up against me. I'm lost in her eyes until they dart down to my mouth, and then I'm looking at her mouth…at her lips, shiny from her pink tongue having just swept across them.

I want my tongue to swipe across them.

"Jay," she says. Her voice is husky with want, and I groan.

"This isn't a good idea," I tell her, knowing what she wants but still not letting her go.

"Just a kiss?" she asks, leaning up on her tip-toes and clasping her hands behind my neck. I hadn't even realized they'd moved from my arms. I'm that lost in her eyes.

"Kate…"

I can kiss her, can't I? There's no harm in a kiss. If it's *just* a kiss. It's everything that comes after the kiss that'll be trouble. My hands are still on her waist and I squeeze, pulling her firmly against me.

"Jay, please kiss me," she begs, and my willpower breaks at the sound of her voice.

I lean my head down, briefly brushing my nose against hers before I claim her lips. They're soft and supple and oh so sweet. I lick the seam of her mouth and she opens on a whimper that instantly makes me hard. She gasps against my mouth just before my tongue presses against hers. She tastes so incredibly sweet, and I wish we were anywhere but here...in a parking lot...where anyone can see us. Then I wish I was anyone but me...a man with a past unworthy of such a pure and perfect woman.

Reality slaps me in the face, and I end the kiss, pulling away from her. Her eyes are glazed over with lust, and her lips are swollen. I want to drag her into her apartment and have my way with her, but I can't. I won't. She deserves so much better than me.

"We can't do this, Kate." I step away from her and over to my bike, stowing the spare helmet.

"Why not?" she asks, her voice now belligerent.

I turn to look at her, and I want to smile at how cute she looks, pouting with her arms folded across her chest, but I know if I did she'd go all spitfire on me, and I can't have that. It'll make it harder to leave...I love it when she gets fired up. After reading those later letters from her, I'd been afraid she'd lost some of her light. But it's still there. My sunshine is still there.

No, not *my* sunshine.

I let out a sigh. "Kate, you know why. I'm no good for you. There's no sense in starting something that isn't gonna be finished. You've got potential, and I'll only bring you down."

"That's bullshit and you know it!"

"It's not bullshit. You're a sweet girl, Kate. You'll meet a nice guy, and he'll be just perfect for you." Just saying the words leaves a bad taste in my mouth, but it's got to be done. "That guy's not me."

"Then why are you even here?"

"I already told you. I wanted to see you and make sure you were okay."

"You could have picked up the damn phone. You didn't have to *move* to California."

I don't have anything to say to that because she's absolutely right. I didn't have to move to California. I could've found a way to reach out to her without relocating across the country on some crazy whim like a psychopath. But I had to see for myself that she was okay. And I had to be near her light. Something about Kate just soothes me, and I'd needed to be close to her.

"You know, Jay, I'm not as innocent, or as naïve, as you seem to think I am." She shakes her head and starts walking past me. When she's right alongside me, she adds, "And you're not as bad as you think you are, either."

I watch as she walks to her building, and I keep watching as she climbs the stairs to her apartment.

"Call me when you get over yourself," she shouts just before she slips in the door.

I shake my head. She's not as innocent as I think she is, eh? Well, that might be the case, but I *am* every bit as bad for her as I say I am. Whether she wants to believe it or not.

Guys like me...we're poison for girls like her.

Chapter Nine

Kate

"Kate?"

"What's up, Case?" I step into the back hallway of the restaurant to take the call because I can't hear well with the din of the activity in the service area.

"My dad is in the hospital. I'm driving home."

Panic grips me. I love Mr. Evans. Casey's dad is one of the sweetest, kindest men I've ever met. He's what I'd always hoped my own father would be like. I'd bonded with Casey's parents over the years when they'd come to visit Case and when they'd secretly call me to check on her and make sure she wasn't pushing herself to hard.

"What's wrong? Is he okay? Do you need me to come home? I'll go with you."

"No! No...it's okay. I'll be okay." But I can tell by her voice that she's not okay and that she won't *be* okay. Casey cherishes her parents.

"Case, I don't want you driving clear across the country by yourself." I'm already grabbing my bag from the staff room and making my way to the back office. Seth, the manager, will just have to deal with it or fire me. It's not like I *need* the money the job brings me. I just wanted something that was mine. Something I'd earned myself, not having to rely solely on my parents' money.

"I can't exactly fly, Kate."

"I know, sweetie. Listen, I'm leaving work now, and I'll ride with you."

"I've already left."

I stop in my tracks. "Casey!"

"You can't afford to take time off school right now, Kate. I know how busy you've been, and you've still got more exams. I knew if I stuck around, you'd try to come with me. I'll be okay. I'll break the trip up. I'll eat well. I promise. I just need to get home to see my dad, and I'll be okay. Everything will be okay." I'm not sure who she's trying to convince—me or herself.

I sag against the wall. My roommate and best friend is *the* most stubborn person on the planet. I can't even believe she's done this. Actually, yes I can. Because she's stubborn! Ugh. Her mother would be furious with me for letting her go alone.

"Casey, you know I don't like this," I tell her, rubbing my temples with my free hand.

"I know, Mom."

I give a small laugh. "Be careful. Call me every hour until you get there, and call me every time you stop. Call me before you go to bed at night and when you wake up. Text me the motel information when you stop. I swear I hate that you're traveling across the country by yourself. This is not smart."

"Now you really sound like my mom."

"Hush. Seriously though, call me or text me or something. I'm gonna be worried sick about you until I hear from you. But don't text me while you're driving. Dammit, your car doesn't have Bluetooth. Do you have your headset? I need you to check in, but I don't want you to be distracted, and I don't want you to have to constantly stop to check in because that's not safe either. Shit, Casey. This is so *not* okay."

"Take a breath, Kate," she laughs. "I will check in with you. I have my headset, it's how I'm talking to you now."

"Okay," I sigh, resigned to the fact that my roommate is traveling cross country solo. "Be careful, please."

"I will, I promise."

"I love you."

"Love you, too. Get back to work and stop freaking out. I'll be fine."

"Okay. I'm sorry about your dad, Case," I add quietly.

I hear her sniffle before she responds. "I know, thanks."

We say goodbye, and I return to the staff room to put away the things I'd grabbed. I can't believe she's doing this. I look at the time on my phone. At eight o'clock at night, no less. I know how much she loves her dad, though, so I guess I'm not entirely surprised. I just wish she would have let me be there for her. She hasn't been home to South Carolina in years—a little bit because of a boy and a lot because of her health issues. Yes, she's from South Carolina, too, but she grew up in Charleston while I grew up in Columbia. It's kind of funny how we were placed together at Stanford, all things considered.

Distracted, I return to work. For the next four hours of my shift, I can't stop thinking about Casey and her dad. I hope Mr. Evans is okay. Casey never did say what was wrong. I don't even know how bad it is. I get one text just before midnight that she's stopping for gas and snacks near Bakersfield, I write back that she'd better stop for the night while she's at it. She sends me back an emoticon that's rolling its eyes, and I shake my head. She's going to push herself until she drops.

I finish my closing duties, and still distracted, make my way out to the parking lot and my car. The sound of a male voice in the darkness saying my name causes me to scream and drop my keys.

"Jesus, Kate. It's me," Jay says, stepping under the glow of a streetlamp. I'm breathing heavy with my hand on my chest as he approaches me. "Hey...what's wrong, Sunshine?" It's not until his thumb swipes my cheek and comes off wet that I realize I'm crying. Which, of course, causes me to cry harder. "Damn," he says, pulling me into his chest. He makes soothing sounds as he rubs my back.

"You didn't call," I say after a while of him holding me. It's been two weeks since our amazing kiss in the parking lot. I hadn't even known if he was still in the state. And now he's here. Holding me.

"I wasn't over myself," he says, and I laugh. I slap his chest, and he pulls away from me, tipping my chin up. "What's this all about? I know you're not this upset over me not calling."

I step away from him and shake my head. "No. My roommate's dad is in the hospital. She left tonight to drive home to Charleston to be with him. I'm worried about her being on the road by herself, and I'm worried about him. She never said what was wrong so I don't know how bad it is. I'm just overwhelmed, I guess."

"Why didn't she fly home?" he asks, apparently addressing the easiest part of that first.

"She has health issues so she can't fly. I told her I'd go with her, but by the time she called me, she'd already left," I tell him, getting frustrated with Casey all over again. "I'm sorry, you're not here to listen to me vent. What's up?"

"Don't apologize. I just wanted to see you."

"Oh...that again, huh?" I roll my eyes and bend to pick up my keys from the ground. "Well, you've seen me," I say once I'm upright, then I turn away from him and walk to my car. I'm not playing games with him. If he wants to see me...to talk to me...to do whatever with me...he needs to get his head out of his ass. I'm not interested in being tossed around like a yo-yo and listening to his self-deprecating monologue. Either he's in or he's out.

"I've missed you." He says it so quietly that I could pretend I hadn't heard it if I wanted to...

But I stop walking and turn to face him again. It's dark, and he's no longer standing under the streetlight, so I can't make out his expression, but his stance reminds me of the vulnerable posture he'd had that first night in the restaurant. He'd looked defeated then, and he seems defeated now.

"Yeah? Well, what are you gonna do about it?"

Chapter Ten

Jay

That's a loaded question.

There are two ways to address this. The way I'd like to...by tossing her hot little sassy ass in the back of her car and letting out years of pent up frustration. Or the way I should...by spending some good, honest time getting to know her again. Yeah, I know that contradicts everything I've been saying to this point. Truth is, I know she's too good for me and I know I'm bad for her, but I've spent the last two weeks trying to stay away from her, and I just can't get her out of my head. She's all I think about. She's been all I thought about for a while now. The only light in my dark days. *My* sunshine.

That's right. *Mine.*

I know I'm bad news, and this will probably end up blowing up in our faces, but I can't help it. I need this girl in my life like I need air to breathe. I'll take as much or as little as I can get.

"I was wondering if you might want to go to lunch again or something?"

"Or something?" she asks, raising an eyebrow and taking a step towards me.

"Yeah," I shrug, walking towards her. "We could go for a movie or have dinner instead."

"What about breakfast?" she asks, the corners of her mouth tilting up in a flirty smile as she comes to a stop in front of me. She runs one of her dainty little fingers, the nail polished in a pale pink, from the scar on my left cheek, down my neck, and straight down my chest, stopping at the waistband of my jeans.

"I like breakfast," I croak. She makes me feel like a teenage virgin. Hell, with how little activity I've had, I might as well be. All the times I've imagined Kate over the years—sweet, innocent Kate—I'd never once painted her as a little seductress. I grab her hand before she decides to go any lower and choose my first option of dragging her to her car.

"You're no fun," she pouts.

"You're...different," I say, still holding her hand.

"How so?" she cocks her head to the side.

I shrug, not knowing how to explain it in a way that won't offend her. I don't know much about females, but I do know that it's important to tread carefully.

"I'm not a teenage girl anymore, Jay. I've practically been on my own for three years now. Of course I'm different. Maybe if you'd bothered to keep in touch, you'd know that."

Ouch, that hurt. Not that I don't deserve her attitude, of course. Because I most certainly do after the way I'd treated her.

And she's right, she's definitely *not* a teenage girl anymore. That's for damn sure. The fact that she's been on her own makes my blood boil. Her parents are some class act for abandoning their only daughter.

You're a class act for abandoning her, too, Spencer. Touché, self, touché.

"You're right. I'm sorry."

She shrugs in response, brushing off this apology in the same way she's done every other one I've offered. What makes me crazy is that her disregarding my apology isn't because she doesn't accept it...it's because she really doesn't seem to hold any grudge against me at all for blowing her off back then. The girl is a saint.

"So...my roommate's out of town. We can go back to my place and watch a movie or something?" She bites the corner of her lip and shifts from one foot to another. I can tell she's nervous, and for some reason this reaction feels more genuine—more Kate—than how forward she was being a moment ago.

"Or something?" I wink and she blushes in response, looking down at her shoes. "Movie, it is," I tell her, and she looks up and smiles.

"I'll see you there," she says, then she turns and walks across the lot to her car. I get on my bike and wait until she's in her car and pulling out before following her out into the street. Five is a swanky place in a nice area, but the neighborhoods Kate has to drive through to get home are a little shady. I don't like the idea of her driving through them at midnight—or later—even though I know she's been doing it a while now.

Even more reason for her to *never* visit my place. Ever.

***

I feel like a high school kid on a first date. No, not even *on* the date yet...picking the girl up for the date. I can almost imagine an imposing father-figure standing before me, staring down at me as I sit on the couch with my back straight as a rod. My boot clad feet are flat on the floor, my knees—bent at a perfect ninety degree angle—are pressed together, and my hands are folded neatly in my lap. I'm not even leaning against the back of the couch. I think I might be sweating, and I definitely feel clammy.

Kate's in the shower. Sitting stock still on the couch is the only thing keeping me from busting down the bathroom door to see what's on the other side. It's been so long since I've been with a woman, and I've never been with one that looks like Kate. I'd messed around with my share of girls in high school and the year or so after graduation. But that's just it...they were all girls. Kate is a woman. A *young* woman, but still a woman. She's twenty-one now, I'm twenty-four. Age-wise, we're perfect. It's everything else that doesn't line up.

I'm a mechanic...she's a med student.

I'm poor...she's rich

I'm going nowhere...and she has so much potential.

My pity train is derailed by the sound of the bathroom door opening. I immediately smell the fruity scent of her soap in the humid air that escapes. It smells good.

"Sorry I took so long," she says as she walks towards the living room, still drying her wet hair with a towel. When she walks out from behind the couch, my jaw drops at the sight of her pajamas. *Is she trying to kill me?* She's wearing tiny blue shorts with a matching tank top that has glittery shit on it. But let's talk about what she's *not* wearing for a moment, shall we? A bra. And judging by the lack of panty lines on her ass as she bends over to look at the shelf near the TV, she's not wearing panties either. "It just feels so good to take a long, hot shower after being on my feet for so long."

Oh, right. She had been saying something when I zoned out on her curves. "It's okay," I tell her, focusing on the first thing she'd said. My freaking voice squeaks just like it did when I'd hit puberty a dozen years ago. I clear my throat. "Nice place." She pauses in her perusal of the shelves and looks over her shoulder at me. The little minx knows exactly what she's doing. I can tell by the tiny smirk on her face.

"Thanks," she says, then looks back at the shelf. "My parents paid for everything, but Casey and I picked it all out and set it up ourselves. Ah-ha!" she plucks a case off the shelf and squats down to place the disc in the player. *Lord, have mercy.* She has the sexiest little ass I've ever seen, and I can see a lot of it right about now.

I clench my hands into fists and shift slightly to relieve the sudden tension in my pants. A tension that's intensified when she flops down on the couch—*right next to me*—and tucks her legs beneath her body. She's just a hairsbreadth away and I can feel the rise and fall of her chest as she breathes. In and out. Up and down. In and out. Up and down.

Thought process not helping!

The opening credits of the movie start. I completely missed the menu screen telling me what we're watching since I'd been stuck in my own private little hell in my head.

Don't look at her breasts.

But they're right there, ever so slightly brushing against my arm. Suddenly, the popular soundtrack of the movie infiltrates my senses, and my eyes dart from her...sparkly shirt...to the television.

"*Halloween?*" I ask her, surprised at her movie selection.

She nods happily, her eyes glued to the screen. "One of my most favorite movies ever."

I smile. My kind of girl. I love a good, old-school horror flick. I never could get into the newer ones that are all about gore and torture and violence. I've seen that kind of shit up close, and there's nothing entertaining about it. Old-school horror movies leave a lot more to the viewers' imaginations. Nothing like scaring the crap out of yourself.

"Oooh!" She pops up off the couch and runs off to the kitchen. "I forgot the popcorn."

"Want me to pause the movie?"

"Nope, I've seen it a thousand times. I'll be right there." I hear the crinkle of a wrapper and the microwave open and close, then the beep of the buttons. "What would you like to drink?" she calls out to me.

"What do you have?" I ask.

"Wine, beer, water, soda."

"Beer's good," I tell her. I can have one now, and it should be out of my system when the movie is over, and I'm ready to ride home in a couple hours.

Another minute or so later, and the microwave beeps. The jack-o-lantern only just left the screen, so she hasn't missed much of the movie. She rustles around in the kitchen some more before finally appearing holding two beer bottles by their necks in one hand and a huge bowl of popcorn in the other. She's obviously got this under control, but I feel like an ass for not getting up and helping her.

I start to rise to help her carry something, but she waves me off. "I'm a waitress, remember?"

"I'm sorry; I should've helped."

"It's no biggie. Sit."

I sit back down and take the offered beer. She cuts off the light and sits next to me again, this time pulling a blanket off the back of the couch and resting it over her lap, before reaching forward and grabbing her beer and the popcorn.

Good. At least with that blanket over her, some of that soft, smooth skin will be covered up and I'll be less tempted to push her down onto the sofa, climb on top of her, and make her mine.

Less being the key word.

Chapter Eleven

Kate

Jeez. I wish he'd just kiss me or touch me *or something* already.

Does he think I'm a virgin? Sure, I might give off the innocent vibe, but I've been with a few guys. I lost my virginity after a party freshman year simply because I wanted to see what the fuss was all about. Casey had said it was a dumb move, that it should be with someone I had feelings for, but I'd looked at it strictly from a scientific perspective—an experiment of sorts. It definitely hadn't been all it was cracked up to be. Sophomore year, I'd dated a guy, Paul, for seven months, and he ended up being number two. Then at the end of last semester, my study partner and I had done the deed to relieve some serious final exam tension. To be honest, with the exception of Paul, my other encounters were very mechanical. It hadn't been fireworks and opera music with Paul, but it had been fun.

What would it be like with Jay? I clenched my thighs together at the thought. Jay must have felt the movement because he glances over at me with a questioning look on his face.

"You okay?" he asks.

I give him a small smile and nod, hoping he doesn't see the blush on my cheeks. Oh, hell. Who am I kidding? I hope he does see the blush and does something about it. But no. He just smiles softly and turns his gaze back to the television.

Jeez. If thinking about him in that way makes my thighs clench, I can only imagine how fooling around would make me feel.

I withhold the frustrated sigh that wants to come out and go back to watching the movie. I see that it's coming upon a scene that may pass as scary to someone who hasn't seen the film a million times before. Jay may know it's one of my favorite movies, but he doesn't know whether or not I still get scared. This might just work in my favor.

Right on cue, I shriek and burrow myself into Jay's side. As if it were rehearsed, he lifts his left arm and curls it around my shoulders, tucking me into his chest. Like a complete gentleman, he doesn't say a word about it. Instead, he starts running his fingers through my slightly damp hair. Mission: accomplished.

After a few minutes of this new, cozy position, I test my luck by getting more comfortable. I move my left arm so my hand is resting across his torso. I feel his abs tense under my fingers—good lord, this man is ripped—and I just barely resist the urge to feel around and name the different muscles. I do spread my fingers wide though, trying to feel as much of him as I can. Aside from riding with him on his bike and our kiss, this is the closest I've been to him, and if he's not going to make a move, I'm at least going to take advantage while I can.

"Kate?" His voice is gruff, and it startles me. I tilt my head up and meet his intense gaze. "What are you doing?"

Busted.

"Just getting comfortable," I say, going for nonchalance but the higher pitch to my voice clearly indicates otherwise.

I'm still looking into his eyes, trapped in his silver stare. His eyebrows draw together and his eyes seem to darken. It looks like he's having some kind of inner struggle. I hope that struggle is about what I think it's about, and I hope it turns out the way I want it to.

"Fuck it," he quietly mutters before angling his body towards mine and pressing me down on the couch. I'm flat on my back, and he's hovering over me, holding his body up with his left arm bent beside my head. I feel his lower body pressed against me and...damn...he's as happy to be here as I am to have him.

He cradles my face in his right hand, and I nuzzle against it. He bites out another curse. "You're killing me, Kate," he whispers.

I rock my hips against him. "Make me feel good, Jay."

He closes his eyes tight as he hisses out a breath. "I don't know how to resist you anymore."

"Then don't," I challenge him.

His eyes pop open, and he looks so deeply into my eyes I could swear he's seeking out my soul. "It's been...a while for me. I don't know..."

"Shh. It's okay," I tell him, framing his face with my hands. "I want this, Jay. I want you. Please."

His pained look nearly breaks my heart. He's been through so much, and I just want him to feel normal...to feel good. I want him to make me feel good, too. I lift my head and kiss him. He doesn't respond at first, letting me take the lead. But soon, he can't hold back, and he presses his lips against mine, taking charge.

The sensations are overwhelming...the feel of his lips against mine—softer than I'd expected from someone so rugged—and quite the contrast to his hard body pressing against mine. He gently grinds himself against me, and I move my hands to the back of his head to pull him closer to me. Still not close enough.

"Oh, God," I breathe as he kisses down my neck. He works his hand down my side, his thumb just barely grazing my breast, causing me to sigh. What delicious torture. He raises himself off me just enough to work my tank top up my body. I lift up to help him out, breaking our kiss only when the top passes between us. I lie back down while he stays raised above me, taking me in with absolute reverence.

"You're so beautiful," he says, before dipping back down to give me a bruising kiss. His hand traces up my side causing my nipples to pebble and goosebumps to spread across my skin. He starts kissing and licking down my neck again, making me squirm. His hand reaches my breast before his mouth and he massages it once...twice...before he takes the tight bud in his mouth. His other hand goes to work on my other breast, and soon his mouth follows. He gives them equal attention—lots of attention—but it still doesn't quench the desire I'm feeling.

His knee is resting between my legs and I subtly scoot down so it's pressing right against my core. A slight shift of my hips and the friction feels so good...so right. Pretty soon, I'm rubbing against his leg in earnest. I'm so close...

"Jay," I moan, finally alerting him to the fact that something *else* is going on here.

He looks down between us and smirks. “That feel good Kate?”

“Mm hmm.”

Jay places his hand between by legs, pressing down with his palm on my pelvic bone to hold me still, conveniently avoiding the throbbing area and stopping my delicious movements. I groan in frustration. The finish line is right there. He chuckles as he rests back on his haunches. “Eager, are we?”

I rock my hips in response, and his smirk disappears. In its place is a heated look of desire. He moves his hand, slipping it inside my shorts. His eyes become hooded as he realizes just how ready I am…how close I’d been. He rubs the sensitive nub with his thumb as he slips a finger inside me. First one, then two. I cry out from the invasion and nearly climax on the spot.

“Please…” I whimper as I close my eyes.

“Please what, Kate?” Jay whispers, his lips right by my ear.

“Don’t stop. Please, don’t stop.”

I’m rocking against his hand, desperate for release, and just as Jay nips my earlobe, I come apart. As the tremors roll through my body, my cries are cut short by Jay pressing his mouth against mine. I ride out the orgasm, and he doesn’t move his fingers until the last tremor wanes.

"Fuck, that was sexy as hell," he says as he pulls away, then presses one more kiss to my lips.

I smile up at him, his face is lit up like a kid in a candy store. I sit up, and he moves back, his expression now curious. This time, I'm the one who smirks.

"Your turn," I tell him as I reach for the button on his jeans.

"No...you don't have to," he says, grabbing my wrist.

"I want to," I smile.

I rise up on my knees and kiss him, silencing any further protest. Then I shake his grip off my wrist. I pull at the hem of his shirt and he gets the idea, lifting it over his head. I press myself against him...bare chest to bare chest...and *ohmygod,* it feels wonderful. I don't remember sex ever feeling this intimate before. As he wraps his arms around me, I make quick work of his jeans, brushing against his erection as I go.

He groans against my mouth, and I smile in response. I pull away and put both hands flat on his chest, pushing him back so he's lying on his back on the couch. His sculpted chest rises and falls with his heavy breaths and the sight encourages me. I glance down at his boxers and lick my lips. I can feel what he's packing in there and I can't wait to see it.

Just as I reach inside his boxer briefs and wrap my hand around him...

the phone rings.

Chapter Twelve

Jay

Fuck.

I tuck myself back into my pants and sit up, looking over to where Kate is pacing the kitchen on her cell phone as I put back on my t-shirt.

"I'm sorry. I have to get it. It's Casey's ringtone" She'd told me before quickly tugging on her tank top and scampering off the couch to get her phone from the kitchen counter.

We were so close.

But it's just as well, we shouldn't be doing anything anyway. A momentary loss of control on my part, but at least we didn't go all the way. At least I hadn't allowed her to reciprocate. That would have likely been the point of no return. I send a silent thanks to her roommate for calling at just the right time.

I rest my elbows on my knees and run my hands over my head, clasping them behind my neck. I guess I need to face the facts...Kate and I are probably never going to be able to be *just* friends. God knows I'm attracted to her, and I know she's attracted to me, too. Is it too late to try to set those feelings aside? Maybe I can help her realize it's in her best interest to do so.

"Sorry about that," Kate says, walking back into the living room. "She's stopped for the night, and I made her promise to call me when she did."

She sits beside me, and I turn to her. "It's okay. I should probably get going anyway."

She frowns as I stand up. "You don't have to leave..."

"It's late," I tell her, pointing at the clock on the DVR. 2:37. I know it's a lame excuse, since it was late when I followed her back to her apartment to begin with.

"Right," she says, getting to her feet. "Thanks for watching the movie with me, even though we didn't get to finish it."

"Maybe some other time," I offer.

She smiles. "That would be nice."

She walks me to her door and frowns again when all I give her is a soft kiss on her forehead. “Good night, Kate.”

“Good night,” she says quietly as she watches me walk away.

I hop on my bike and fasten my helmet, feeling like a total asshole. Taking a quick look up at her apartment, I catch the lights turn off one-by-one. I’m caught between wishing I was still up there and knowing that I shouldn’t be.

She deserves better than you, I remind myself as I start my bike and pull out of the lot.

Maybe if I repeat that mantra enough, it’ll keep me away. Maybe if I say it to her enough, it’ll keep *her* away. Somehow, I doubt that though. Kate’s too stubborn—too good—to see just how bad I am for her. Doesn’t she realize she doesn’t have a future with someone like me? She can’t ever take me home to meet her parents. She can’t take a guy like me to those fancy banquets and shit doctors and other rich people attend.

She has no future with me.

None.

The sooner she realizes it, the better.

***

I’m wiping down a custom chopper I’ve just changed the oil on when my phone vibrates in my pocket. I let out a frustrated sigh, certain that it's probably Kate calling me for the third time today. It's been two days since I left her at her apartment. I'm trying to stay away, but she's relentless...calling a few times each day. I feel bad letting the calls go to voicemail, but I'm trying to put distance between us. I'm no good, and she needs to get that. Tough love or whatever. I know I came to California to see her, but not with the intention of starting something physical...just a friendship. At least initially.

I look at my phone and am relieved to see it's not Kate but Sean, my best friend from back home.

"Hey, man, what's going on?"

"Nothing, bro. Just checking in, seeing how things are going."

"Everything's all right," I tell him, dropping the cloth on the work bench and stepping outside the garage. My boss, Leroy, knows I'm a decent worker, so he doesn't mind when I take a quick break here and there. Mostly because I never take them.

"How's Kate?" I let out a sigh. Leave it to Sean to go for the jugular. "That good, huh?"

"Kate's Kate. She's amazing and perfect..."

"And everything you shouldn't have...blah blah blah," Sean says, cutting off my usual diatribe.

"Right." I kick at a small rock in the parking lot and cringe as it heads towards the open garage bay. I relax when it stops short of the bike I'd just finished working on.

"Look, man, why the hell are you even out there?"

"You know why." He's the only one who knows the whole story of me and Kate.

"But if you're going to keep sabotaging yourself, then what's the point? I get that you think she's too good for you. Hell, she probably is."

"Thanks, bro."

"I'm not finished. You're self-deprecation is really starting to get on my nerves, Spencer."

I laugh. "I love it when you use big words on me."

"I'm serious, Jay. You're a good guy who's been dealt a shit hand and you just keep playing it anyway. I get that your parents putting you down all the time fucked you up, okay? But you have a chance to start over...start fresh. It pisses me off that you're not taking it. It pisses me off that you're going to let a few bad years dictate the rest of your life. You're better than that."

Now that pisses me off. Those "few bad years" *are* going to dictate the rest of my life. "Listen here," I start, but he cuts me off again.

"No, *you* listen here...you have a choice and you're making a shitty one. You're conforming to what you think society thinks of you instead of manning up and being who you really want to be. You think that girl sees you the way you see yourself? The way your parents saw you? Hell, no. She wouldn't have kept writing to you all that time if she had. But if you keep treating yourself like that, other people are gonna start doing it, too. Get the fuck over your shit, man."

I want to reach through the phone and choke my friend...but I know the asshole is right.

"So you up for a road trip to Sturgis this year?" Sean asks after a few moments of silence.

"That's a long ass road trip," I tell him, appreciating how quickly we can flip from wanting to punch one other to making plans.

"Says the guy who rode his bike across the country," he responds dryly.

I laugh. "Exactly, so I know."

"Come on, dude. It'll be a kick ass time. If you're still in California, we can meet in Kansas or some shit."

"Okay, deal. When else am I gonna get to have a road trip with my best friend now that he's all domesticated?" I joke, certain that Sean's wife, Julia, is not going to be thrilled about him riding to South Dakota.

"Stop, you're making me emotional," Sean laughs.

I see Leroy step out of his office in the back. "Hey, man, I'm at work so I'd better go. I'll call you this weekend, and we can talk about Sturgis."

"Sounds good. I'll have some info ready. Later, buddy."

I hang up the phone and give a nod to Leroy, then step back to the custom chopper I'd been polishing before Sean's call came through. As much as I don't want to admit it...Sean's right.

If I don't believe in myself, who the hell will?

Chapter Thirteen

Kate

I set my phone on the coffee table and sigh. Looking up at the ceiling, I will myself not to cry. I've already done enough of that.

Jay is avoiding me. Two days I've been calling him and no response. Sometimes the voicemail picks up after only one ring, like he's declined the call instead of letting it ring out. I left a voicemail yesterday because I'd wanted to see him again…pick up where we'd left off at my apartment the night before. Then I got the news from Casey this morning that her father had passed away. Now I simply need a friend.

I thought that's what Jay and I had set out to be…friends. Sure, the other night may have complicated that a bit...but our attraction to one another is unavoidable and surely it was going to culminate at some point. It was to be expected. I just can't believe he'd play the avoidance game. I thought we'd made progress as friends even before we'd gotten intimate. It's kind of funny considering all the times we've been together he's been so concerned about not being good enough for me.

Way to prove your point.

Message received.

I have an exam in one of my classes that I absolutely cannot miss and hadn't been able to reschedule, so I'm not able to fly out for Casey's dad's services. It breaks my heart that I can't be there for my friend, but I know her mother will take good care of her. She needs this time with her mom anyway. There's been too much distance between them—physical distance. Casey hasn't been home to South Carolina in the almost three years we've been here. Not that I'm one to talk. The difference is...Casey's parents actually want her there.

But that's a wound for another time.

The wound I'm focusing on now is the one that Jay Spencer has left on my heart. No, I'm not in love with the guy. That would be foolish considering we barely know one another. But, besides Casey, he's been the only real friend I've had here in California. Pathetic, right? Considering we've only just reunited. I was real with him though, through my letters years ago and our recent talks. It was different from the acquaintanceships I keep with fellow students for the sake of appearances and study groups. They're all convenience friends...convenient for the sake of school, not my personal life.

Not to mention Jay is gorgeous and sexy and the things he can do with his fingers and tongue...

I digress...

I lean back against the comforting couch cushions and close my eyes. Try as I might, I just can't stop my thoughts from turning to Jay. The way he makes me feel...physically and emotionally...it completes me.

He completes me.

How cliché.

But seriously...he's everything I hadn't known I'd been missing in my life.

I don't know why he even moved to California if he's going to act like a big freaking baby and hide from me when things get a little too hot for him to handle. What a chicken shit. He came here for me, for crying out loud. Then he makes the grand gesture and cowers...what the hell is that about?

I open my eyes and sit up straight. No. I'm not going to let him pull that. If he wants to back away from me and pretend that we're nothing...not even friends...he can do it to my face. I look at the clock and see that it's almost four. I never asked, but I assume Jay works nine to five, so I've got time to get to his shop and patiently wait for him to clock out so we can have a little come to Jesus meeting.

I think he'd said his boss's name was Leroy, so I type "Leroy" and "motorcycle repair shop" into the search engine on my phone. Almost immediately I have a hit for a shop in San Jose.

"Bingo!" I jump up from the couch and grab my bag from the table by the door. I slip my feet into my flip flops and do a quick face check in the small mirror over the table. I'd been crying, so I make sure my eyes aren't too puffy and I don't have snot on my face. My hair could use some work, but otherwise I look okay, so I pick up my keys and open the apartment door, stepping right out into a firm, solid chest.

"What the...?" I look up and my eyes widen. Jay. Here. On my doorstep.

"Going somewhere?" he asks with a smirk.

Oh no, he doesn't. He doesn't get to act all cute. I lift up my chin in defiance. "Yeah, I was going somewhere."

He takes a step back and raises his arm as if he's letting me pass. "Don't let me stop you."

I narrow my eyes at him and take a step forward so we're only about a foot apart. Then I point my finger right into his sternum. "I was going to see you."

His eyebrows draw together. "See me? Where?"

"Leroy's," I tell him, giving him a smirk of my own.

His eyes widen, and he starts shaking his head. "You can't go over there."

"Well, obviously. Because you're here."

"No, Kate. I mean anytime. That's not a good neighborhood, and you don't need to be wandering around it."

I roll my eyes. I'm so sick of this right side/wrong side of the tracks crap. I've volunteered in places as bad as or worse than what he's trying to protect me from. "Whatever. What are you doing here, anyway?"

"I came to apologize."

"Oh, yeah?" I ask, raising my eyebrows. Maybe I won't have to lay it into him after all. Or maybe I still will; I haven't decided. I let out a sigh, deflating from my tense posture and open my apartment door again. "Come in." He follows me inside and I offer him a drink, which he declines. He takes a seat on the sofa, and I sit in the armchair diagonal to it, not ready to be next to him on *that* couch yet. I look at him expectantly, and he finally takes the hint and starts talking.

"I'm sorry for not taking your calls. I talked to Sean today, and he sort of put things into perspective for me. I wanna be a better guy...a better man..."

“You’re already a good guy, Jay,” I tell him, leaning forward in my seat.

“I know you think that—”

“I don’t think it, I know it,” I tell him, my tone not leaving room for negotiation.

“I know, Kate. I know.” His shoulders rise and fall with the weight of his sigh. “But I’ve spent the last several years being told I was a good-for-nothing, piece of shit—by my parents and myself. I need to convince myself that’s not true. I…” It pains me to hear how poorly he thinks of himself, and I hate to see him struggling so much with his words. “I need to believe in myself, Kate. The way that you believe in me. So I can be a better man. For you. I want to be a better man for you.”

My heart melts at his words. He wants to be a better man for me? He wants to believe in himself? Gosh, if he could only see what I see. But that’s the problem, isn’t it? He can’t and he needs to.

I can’t wait to show him.

I get up from the chair and walk over to where he’s sitting, certain he can see the moisture in my eyes but not giving a damn. I kneel down in front of him and wrap my arms around his body, hugging him tight. I rest my head on his shoulder and squeeze. He raises his arms slowly, then wraps them around me and lets out a relieved sigh.

"I know you already know *I* think you're pretty amazing, but I'll do whatever I can to help *you* believe that, too."

He squeezes me tighter and whispers "thank you" into my hair, and I think that maybe, just maybe, everything will work out.

Chapter Fourteen

Jay

Things got better...easier...between Kate and me after I finally decided to take down my walls and let her in. We had a good talk that day in her apartment, and many more since. I know it sounds crazy, but I can actually feel the positivity rolling off her. She just has this energy and I'm sucking up every bit of it I can.

My sunshine. My light.

We've kissed some more, but that's it. I'd told her straight out that I don't want to go further until I'm sure my head is on straight. I'm getting there though. Which is great since she's getting harder and harder to resist. The things she does with her mouth when we're making out are amazing, not to mention her hot little body. I can't wait to touch and kiss every last bit of it.

Kate's roommate is back, and there's some sort of ex-boyfriend or guy friend drama going on. Kate's been pretty wrapped up in taking care of her friend the last couple days, and taking final exams—it seems like she's always taking exams—so when I'm not at work, Sean and I have been laying down the details for our road trip to Sturgis in August. We've got plenty of time, but we're not the only guys planning on riding to the rally, so we need to make sure we've got our route mapped and our hotel reservations in place. It would suck to land at a motel with no vacancy. The more Sean and I talk about the trip, the more excited I get about it.

"I'm thinking about leaving early, riding down to L.A., and taking Route 66 to Oklahoma," I tell Sean, following the route on the map with my finger.

"That's quite the detour, bro. It's a killer idea, though. Wish I could make that part of the trip with you."

"Why can't you?" I ask, already knowing the answer. This trip is going to take weeks as it is, add a cross-country trip to that and Julia is sure to have a fit. She's a cool chick and all, but what wife wants her husband to be out joyriding with his best friend for almost a month?

"Jules would have my ass if I even suggested it." I hear him exhale and know that he's smoking a cigarette. I wish he'd quit, but the fool has been at it since junior high. I doubt he's going to stop now.

I laugh. "I'm surprised she's even letting you go to Sturgis."

"She's not *letting* me do anything. I'm my own man. She's got her books and shit and goes to all those things where she meets authors and people as crazy as she is...I've got my bike."

"And those things where you meet bike builders and people as crazy as you are?"

He laughs. "Exactly."

"You want to meet around OKC?" I ask him.

"I think Amarillo would be more even. And there's more of a straight shot north to Sturgis from there, too. Through Colorado."

I look on the old fashioned, huge U.S. map I have spread out on the table before me and see what he's talking about. The route makes more sense than the one from Oklahoma City. "We'll need to map out gas stations along the way."

"We should probably grab a pull-behind or two, stow some extra shit in 'em. Maybe some extra gas, just in case. A lot of these routes are pretty desolate and we don't want to get screwed."

I groan internally. Nothing badass about towing a pull-behind, but we've got to be practical, no matter how uncool it may be. Sean's right. We don't want to end up out of gas in the middle of nowhere. A planned gas stop may be closed, we could hit traffic, weather…you never know.

"Good idea. Let's plan on that."

"So how's it going with Kate?"

This time I groan out loud. He's held it in this long, I'll give him that much. "It's going."

"Did you get over yourself?" he chuckles, loving how uncomfortable he's making me. I hate talking about feelings and shit, and I about overdosed on it with him the last time.

"I did," I admit.

"That's my boy," he whoops. "You gonna give it a go?"

"We're gonna try. She believes in me." I say that last part quietly, almost hoping he doesn't hear me.

"Well, I like her already," Sean says. "I can't wait to meet her. You bringing her to Sturgis?"

I laugh out loud at that. Yeah, I can just picture Kate at Sturgis in her pastel clothes and fancy shoes. Don't get me wrong, she'd be sexy as hell in a paper bag, but the people of Sturgis are a whole different breed. I've never been, but I've seen pictures. Half-dressed women and lots of black, leather, and denim. She's too prim and proper for all that, and I wouldn't change her for a minute, I love her just the way she is.

Wait...love?

No.

Maybe?

Could I love her?

I sure as hell feel something for her.

"Sean...how did you know? With Jules? How did you know she was the one?"

Sean's quiet for a minute, and I can tell I just threw him for a loop. "You serious right now?"

"I don't know."

"It's different for everyone, bro. With Jules, I just knew. It was so obvious it just couldn't be explained as anything else. It hits you like a fucking Mack truck, dude."

"Must not be love if I had to ask then, huh?"

"Maybe, maybe not. You've got so much shit in your head, you haven't allowed yourself to relax and go with the flow. I bet once you do, it'll hit you," he says. "If that's what it is," he adds as an afterthought.

"I guess."

"So I take it Kate won't be coming to Sturgis?"

I'm grateful to Sean for changing the subject. "Not her scene."

"Well, I can't wait to meet her," he says, and I can tell he means it.

"Same here. Maybe after she graduates," I tell him, even though I have no clue what Kate wants to do after she graduates. All I know is she plans to go to medical school, even though she doesn't want to, but I don't know where. Shouldn't you know something like that about the person you're in a relationship with? Are we even in a relationship? What if she chooses a med school in another city? Am I supposed to just follow her? I followed her here...does she expect me to now? I'm getting way ahead of myself.

"Earth to Spencer."

I shake the thoughts from my head. "Sorry, man."

"It's all good. I remember when Jules and I first got together. I spaced out a lot," he chuckles.

I frown. I hadn't been there for that. I wish I could have seen my best friend acting a total fool in love with his girl. I'd only met Julia a handful of times before I left South Carolina. Even in those brief moments, I could tell how much Sean loved her and how much she loved him. They looked at each other with stars in their eyes and shit.

Do Kate and I look at each other like that?

“Hey, man. Sorry to cut this short but Jules just got home with dinner. We’ll talk next week?”

“Yeah. I’ll look for a pull-behind.”

“Me, too. Later, bro.”

“Later.”

I end the call and as usual, my thoughts drift to Kate. Will I ever be able to let go of my past enough to just be in the present? Will I ever be able to fully *feel* anything with her until I do?

Chapter Fifteen

Kate

The past few days have been...interesting. I'd come home one day and unexpectedly found Casey's long lost best friend, Decker, asleep on our doorstep, and Casey fast asleep inside the apartment. She'd just arrived home, and turns out, he'd followed her home from South Carolina. Though, technically he'd flown, so he arrived earlier than she did. I'd agreed to let him stay at the apartment, knowing that having him near was the only way he and Casey would work their shit out.

But poor Decker...he was going stir crazy being stuck in the apartment all day while Casey was at work. Evidenced by the way he'd just grabbed her keys from her hand and ran out of the apartment like a bat out of hell when she arrived home from work.

"What the hell just happened?" Casey asks, standing in the doorway.

I laugh at the stunned look on her face. "He's been like a caged animal all day. Practically bouncing off of every surface in this place. We played two games of Monopoly, Casey. Two! Do you know how much time it takes to play two games of Monopoly? I was about to ask Dr. Vasquez if he had any ketamine." Dr. Vasquez, who is a veterinarian, is our neighbor.

Casey laughs with me. "Thanks for hanging out with him today."

I give her a sad smile. "You know, you could just tell him," I suggest. Lord knows it would make everything so much easier if Casey would just disclose her health situation to Decker.

"No, I can't," she sighs.

"What's the big deal?" I ask, ignoring her responding glare. "Seriously, Casey. You can use all the support you can get."

"That's the thing!" she shouts, raising her hands and slapping them down on her hips. "I already get babied enough by you and my mom. I don't need anyone else tiptoeing around me. I'm fine."

"You're *not* fine. But whatever. You know I'm not going to say anything. But *you* should. He deserves to know."

“Whatever,” She shakes her head and storms over to the couch, plopping down on it with a thud. I shake my head at her performance and finish cleaning up the mess in the kitchen from mine and Decker’s snacks earlier.

“That was dramatic,” I say as I sit down beside her and take one of her hands. “You know I only care about you and want what’s best?” She nods but doesn’t say anything, so I continue. “Decker cares about you and wants what’s best for you, too.”

“Drop it,” she says as she pulls her hand away from me.

“Fine,” I sigh. She is the most hard-headed person I know. I take the nail file out of my nail bag and begin filing my nails. If she doesn’t want to talk about it, I’m not going to make her.

“So...what’s up with you? You’ve been acting weird lately.”

Well, how’s that for karma?

“Nothing’s up with me.” I don’t bother looking at the “yeah, right” look on her face. I can feel it from here.

“You can play nonchalant all you want, but something’s up with you.” She snatches the file from my hands and starts doing her own nails. Bitch.

“I was using that.”

“Start talking,” she says.

I start chewing the inside of my lip—a telltale sign of my nerves, which Casey is completely aware of. I see her eyes widen. Great.

"I've been talking to a guy," I say quietly, not sure how much of mine and Jay's story I want to unveil. I know what she'll probably think, and I don't want her to jump to conclusions about him.

"What?!" she asks. She drops the file and turns to face me. "Tell me everything!"

"It's nothing," I say, rolling my eyes. "He's totally not my type." I try to downplay it, hoping she'll back off. She tilts her head to the side, and I can see her wheels turning. She's not going to back off. I'll need to put her out of her misery...fast. "He rides a motorcycle. He's a mechanic," I shrug, trying to make it seem like it's not a big deal and instantly feeling terrible that I've just put Jay in a box.

Casey's eyes widen, but she still says nothing. I worry that she's judging him, and I don't like that idea. Not at all. "He came into the restaurant a couple months ago. We talked a little bit, but he was there with his friends so we couldn't talk much. He gave me his number before he left, and we've sort of been texting ever since. Sometimes we talk on the phone."

There...that was a slight stretch of the truth. No, he didn't come to the restaurant with friends, but what would Casey think if I'd told her he came there just for me? She'd want to know more, and I'm not ready to tell her more. I'm also not about to tell her I'd ridden on his motorcycle and invited him inside our apartment. That we'd gotten hot and heavy right on this very couch. She'd freak out.

I start to blush under Casey's scrutiny. "Say something!" I shriek, slapping at her arm. She grimaces, and I feel bad; I might have hit her harder than I'd meant to.

"You've been busy!" she says after a moment, smiling.

I can feel my face heat even more. "It's not like that."

"Then what's it like? Are you trying to tell me you guys aren't sexting?"

"Casey!" I yell, slapping her again. I can't believe she just went there!

"Ouch! What?" she asks, rubbing her arm.

"Stop it!"

"Not until you tell me more. Where does he work? What's he look like? I don't even know where to begin!"

Here's the inquisition I'd been hoping to avoid. Keep is simple, Kate. "He works at a repair shop in San Jose. He's tall, dark and handsome."

She rolls her eyes at my lack of details. "What's his name?"

"Jay."

She nods, processing this new information. "Do you like him?"

"Yeah," I answer truthfully, looking down. "But it's never going to be anything, so it doesn't matter."

She takes my hand and tugs at it until I look at her. "Why would you think that? You're amazing, beautiful, smart..."

I laugh, even if I am those things, I know it's not enough. "Yeah, but we're so different. He's totally hot, and he knows it. He and his friends are boisterous and out of control. He's my complete opposite."

While I was working a couple nights ago, Jay had stopped in to the restaurant with some of the guys he works with. I was working the bar, and he'd kept his friends away from me and seated at a high-top table across the room. I didn't get the chance to interact with them at all, and it had seemed as though Jay designed it that way...that he was trying to keep us separated, so I didn't push it. He'd told me that he missed me and needed to see me. It made my heart melt. The whole situation had clued me in on just how different the two of us are, though. I watched him off and on that night, noting how different he was when he was in his element like that...in his natural habitat so-to-speak. He didn't behave that way with me; he was more guarded. It was as though I was holding him back from who he truly was.

"Hey, you're hot, too," Casey says, breaking me from my thoughts. "And you know what they say, 'opposites attract.'"

"That's so cliché." I sigh. I start digging through my nail bag to find the perfect color to paint my nails.

"If it's meant to be, it'll be," Casey says, and I laugh. Now *that's* cliché.

"Ha-ha," I say dryly. I pull two colors out of the bag, trying to change the subject. "Passion Pink or Radiant Rose?"

She points to Passion Pink. Figures. "Look, if he doesn't appreciate what's right in front of him, that's his problem. You're a great catch and it's his loss."

"It's complicated, Case. I just don't know." When she narrows her eyes at me, I know I've said a little too much.

"What aren't you telling me?"

"Nothing. I told you everything that's relevant." I look away from her and start painting my nails. Hoping she doesn't ask another question.

"Kate?"

"Yeah?"

"What aren't you telling me?" I ignore her, acting like the coward I most certainly am. "You really like this guy, don't you?"

I close my eyes tight. She hit the nail right on the head with that one. I take a deep breath and decide to be honest with my roommate. I look up and tell her, “More than I can even explain.”

She nods as if she was expecting this response, though I’m not sure how. “Okay. That’s good. If you care about him, then he can’t be a bad guy, right? You’re an excellent judge of character. I’m sorry I jumped to conclusions.”

“Thank you,” I say, relaxing for the first time since we started this conversation. “He’s a really great guy.”

She smiles a genuine smile, and I decide I’m glad I told her about Jay. “Good. He better take good care of you.”

Given the opportunity, Jay would take excellent care of me. I know it. If he’d just give himself the benefit of the doubt.

“What is it?” Casey asks, noting my change in mood.

“It’s nothing,” I tell her, shaking my head. I love Casey to death but she wouldn’t understand. Would she? Maybe, of all people, Casey would understand. She *is* a psychology major. She has a decent understanding of human behavior. Maybe she’d understand. Or maybe she’d really freak out. Maybe the things she’s learned in class about Jay’s “type” would send her running. Maybe she’d tell my parents. No, she’d never do that.

"Kate?"

I sigh. Maybe I can tell her just a little bit to feel her out and see how she responds? Here goes nothing... "Jay–"

I'm interrupted by Decker barreling through the front door carrying about ten grocery bags. I have to admit I'm a little relieved that this conversation is over.

Casey gets up to help him but quickly turns back to me and says, "We're not finished here."

"I figured," I say, collecting my nail supplies and getting the heck out of there. If there's anything I want to do less than talk about my relationship and history with Jay, it's watch the two lovebirds that don't know they're lovebirds dance around each other.

Chapter Sixteen

Jay

I can't believe I'm going to a club. A dance club at that. I could hardly believe it when Kate asked me to meet her and her friends there. I'm still not sure I believe it. The guys at work razzed me when I told them where I was going after I'd declined their offer to hit the pool hall tonight. The pool hall was much more my speed, but Kate...yeah, need I say more?

I've only seen her once in the past week and, like tonight, we weren't alone. A few nights ago, the guys and I were at the pool hall, which is only a ten minute drive from Five. I knew Kate was working, and I missed her, so as we were leaving, I'd told the guys I was going to Five. I should have just told them I was going home. I hadn't thought they'd want to join me. When we arrived, I'd spotted Kate working behind the bar and sat them as far away from her as I could. I knew they'd roughhouse, and I didn't want her to be subjected to it. Johnny and Tom are cool guys, but Steven can get a little out of control.

When I walked up to the bar, her chocolate brown eyes lit up, and her smile was wide. I could tell I'd made her night just by being there. I'm not sure I've ever had that effect on anyone. It made me feel superhuman. I'd felt bad for not introducing her to the guys, and they'd teased me about "the babe at the bar" and how they'd keep coming back to a stuck up place like this if the service always looked that good. That had just cemented for me why I hadn't introduced them to Kate. I'm not ashamed of my new friends, or Kate, I just knew they wouldn't behave.

So here I sit—sipping on the eight dollar beer I can't really afford, but need to alleviate my nerves—looking through the crowd, trying to spot her. On my right is Johnny, and on my left is Tom. Neither one of them would miss the opportunity to see me at a dance club. I have to say, though, they clean up nice and, fortunately for me, Steven couldn't make it. The three of us are dressed up in nice jeans and long-sleeved, button-down shirts. I'd even scrubbed the grease out from under my nails.

Finally, I see her blonde hair across the room and rise from my stool to go to her, leaving the expensive ass beer on the bar without saying a word to the guys. Hell, they're not stupid. They know what's up whether I care to admit it or not.

I wade through the crowd and finally make it to Kate. God, she's so beautiful. She must have cut her hair recently, and now the blonde locks frame her face perfectly. As I approach the table, I see a guy set down some drinks. Kate nods off to the side, and the guy walks off in that direction.

"Hey," she says with a big smile when she sees me.

"You cut your hair," I say, toying with a lock as I step in to kiss her cheek.

"You like?" she asks shyly, touching her hair with her hand.

"I love," I tell her, thinking more about the blush rising on her cheeks than her hair at the moment.

"I had it up at the restaurant, otherwise you would have seen it the other night."

"You look beautiful," I tell her as I look at her outfit. She's wearing dark, snug jeans with a sparkly purple top.

"Thanks."

"Have you been here long?" I ask when I see that there are three drinks on the table in front of her.

"An hour maybe?" I frown, I've been here nearly as long. How did I not spot her until now? "What's wrong?"

I shake my head. "Nothing, I've just been hanging out at the bar. I didn't realize you were already here."

"I texted you," she says. I pull my phone out and see that she texted me about forty-five minutes ago. With all the vibrations from the music, I must not have felt it buzz.

"Sorry," I say, tucking the phone back in my pocket.

"It's okay; you're here now," she says smiling, putting her hand over mine.

"Hey," I lean in so she can hear me over the music. "My friends are at the bar with my drink. I'm going to go get it, and I'll be right back." She nods, and I head back to the bar.

"Your lady friend arrive?" Johnny asks.

"She did," I nod, grabbing my beer off the bar top and turning to go back to Kate.

"So that's how it's gonna be?" Tom says.

I stop walking and sigh. I should have known these two weren't going to make it easy for me. "What do you want?"

"We want to meet your friend," Johnny says.

I look at the two goofballs in front of me. They may be a little rough around the edges, but they *are* my friends. They're good guys. If I want to make a go at something with Kate, I should introduce her to my friends, right? I'm here tonight to meet *her* friends. I guess it's only fair she meet mine.

I give an almost imperceptible nod before turning around, but Johnny and Tom see it, and they hurry after me. When we reach Kate's table, that guy is back, and with him is a girl. The guy looks athletic. He's tall with reddish brown hair and introduces himself as Decker. The girl, a short brunette, introduces herself as Casey. I recognize her as the girl I'd seen leave Kate's apartment the day we'd met for lunch. I shake both their hands and smile politely, introducing Tom and Johnny.

There, that wasn't so bad. We've met the friends. One milestone under our belts...only a million more to go.

Shortly after joining their table, Casey drags Kate off to dance.

"She's had a few," Decker says, staring after Casey longingly. "If she realizes she's dancing in a club she'll probably die of shock." He finishes his drink and heads off to the dancefloor after them.

"He's got it bad," Johnny says, and I nod in agreement.

"So does our boy here," Tom adds.

I don't deny it, there would be no point. I probably look as lovesick as Decker does. The guys and I make small talk while I watch Kate dance with Casey. Decker dances with them off and on, staying nearby and not taking his eyes off Casey. Kate was right, those two need to sort their shit out.

After several songs, Decker approaches the table and grabs an unopened water bottle. "Hey, man," he nods before he chugs the water.

"So what's up with you and Casey?" I ask as he sets the empty water bottle down on the table.

"What's up with you and Kate?"

I smirk, smart guy. "Kate says you and Casey are 'just friends,' but I see the way you look at her."

He looks at me oddly before answering. "She's my best friend. Has been my whole life."

I laugh. "Kate says you two only just recently reconnected after being apart for a few years."

"Yeah, so?" he asks, defensively.

"Does she know you're in love with her?"

His eyes widen. Bingo. "Excuse me?" His eyes dart to Johnny and Tom who aren't paying us a bit of attention. They've got their eyes on a bachelorette party across the club.

"She's special, yeah?" I ask.

His eyes find Casey on the dance floor, and when they do his face transforms. Yeah, he's a goner. "She's everything."

I know the feeling, buddy. I know the feeling.

Chapter Seventeen

Kate

Lucky for me, Casey's reaction to Jay after finally meeting him isn't nearly as bad as I had anticipated it would be. She'd simply whispered in my ear that he was hot and left it at that. I think the alcohol helped, though. I'm not comfortable with her drinking a lot, and I've been trying to slip her water here and there. But I know she's going to do whatever she wants to do regardless of the consequences, so the best I can do is keep an eye on her and hope my instincts about Decker remain true, and he takes good care of her.

Jay's friends, Tom and Johnny, are real nice guys. They don't seem nearly as crazy as they did the night they came to Five, but they told me that was mostly their friend Steven, who wasn't with them tonight, and apologized for getting rowdy.

I learn that Johnny is Jay's age, twenty-four, and is a total player. He spends most of the conversation talking about every "piece of ass" that walks by. Every time he says it, though, he bashfully looks at me and apologizes for his language. I can't wait for him to fall head over heels. I hope I get to see it.

Tom is a little older, twenty-seven, and is divorced with two little girls. The way he talks about them, it's clear they're his entire world. I've never seen that look of pride and love from my own father, but I can recognize it in a doting dad. I'd spend enough time around Casey's dad to know that.

Thinking about Casey's dad brings tears to my eyes, and I'm thankful she and Decker are out on the dance floor again. If she were sitting here, I wouldn't be able to contain them—not with all the alcohol I've imbibed—and she doesn't need that. Not when she's out there having so much fun. I couldn't understand why Decker had wanted to take Casey to a club—a freaking club!—but now I get it. Seeing the smile on her face makes this uncomfortable evening worth it.

Eventually Casey and Decker join us at the table, and the six of us make pleasant conversation for another thirty minutes or so before they all start dropping like flies. Tom is the first to go since he's picking up his girls in the morning. Johnny finds someone receptive to his charms and leaves with her a little while later. Next up, I'm sure, will be Casey and Decker. I haven't missed the sexy eyes those two have been throwing back and forth all night, and I really, really don't want to go home with them.

I put my hand on Jay's thigh and lean in to whisper in his ear. "Can I go home with you?"

His eyes dart to mine; they're wide in…fear? *What the hell?* "I don't think that's a good idea."

"Why not?" I frown, giving him my best sad eyes.

"It's just not a good idea, Kate. I'll take you home if you need a ride, but I don't want you coming back to my place."

I jolt back in my seat, stunned. *Well, that kinda hurt.* "It's okay," I tell him, brushing off his brush off. "I'll just ride home with Casey and Decker."

His eyes narrow on me, most likely picking up on my chilly tone. He can get right over it.

"Kate—"

I ignore him, turning to Casey and Decker who are lost in their own little dreamy staring contest. "You guys ready?"

Casey looks at me first. "Yeah, we're ready." She takes Decker's hand and starts pulling him to the door.

I pick up my drink and drain the last bit, then I look at Jay. "Thanks for coming out tonight." I give him a quick smile and follow my friends.

I don't get far before Jay's hand is on my wrist. I know it's him because I can feel the zing pulsing up my arm from his touch. Only Jay affects me that way. I stop moving and sigh when I feel him behind me. I wish he'd stop sending me all these damn mixed signals.

"What's wrong?" he asks as I turn to face him.

I let out a sigh and decide to be honest with him. "You're giving me whiplash, Jay. One minute you act interested and the next you don't. We've been having a good time tonight, hanging out with our friends and everything. Then you get all freaked out when I ask to go back to your place. I don't know what to think anymore. I'm tired of the back and forth. Just...call me when you know what it is you want...when you're ready or whatever."

I pull my wrist away from his grasp and he releases it immediately. After one last look at him, I turn and walk out, my thoughts raging in my head. I thought we'd been making progress. When he came to the apartment that night before Casey came home and we talked...I thought things were going to be different. I thought he was going to stop distancing himself from me. Looks like I was wrong.

I step out into the night, and the chill in the air takes my breath away. My top is not exactly skimpy, but it is short sleeved and plenty appropriate for inside the hot club. Not so appropriate for the chilly spring night. I cross my arms and rub my hands up and down my upper arms to warm up as I crane my neck, looking for Casey and Decker. There are quite a few people outside of the club now, probably waiting for cabs. I spot my friends a few yards away and head in that direction.

"Kate! Wait!" I roll my eyes and pick up my pace. I'd had an okay buzz going, and he's totally ruining it. "Kate!" People are looking now, including Casey and Decker. Great. I stop so abruptly that Jay bumps into my back. His hands go to my waist to keep me from falling forward.

I turn to face him, angry now and feeling more than a little humiliated. I'm not a fan of being the center of attention and, right now, most of the people standing outside the club are looking at us. "What?" I demand, crossing my arms.

"I'm sorry," he says, looking properly chastised. "It's not that I don't want to be with you, because I do, Kate. I want to be with you so bad. It's just my apartment isn't in a great area and it's small..."

This is really *just* about his apartment? Does he really think I care about where he lives?

"Jay...that doesn't bother me."

"Well, it bothers me. It's not a safe area, Kate."

I step close to him and put my hands over his cheeks. "Jay, I don't care. I don't care what your apartment looks like or what neighborhood you live in. I know those things don't define you, and I know you'll keep me safe. I just want to spend more time with you. I want to see the parts of your life you keep from me. Trust me, Jay. Trust me not to judge you."

He closes his eyes and takes a deep breath. When he opens them again, I know I have him. He gives me a soft nod and leans in to kiss my forehead, then wraps his arms around my shoulders and holds me for a minute. "Come on, let's go tell your friends you're coming with me."

I look up at him and grin, barely able to contain my excitement. I'm going to Jay's apartment! There's a definite bounce in my step as I head over to Casey and Decker and tell them they've got the apartment to themselves tonight. Both of their eyes widen in surprise, but I just wink at Casey and tug on Jay's hand, pulling him through the parking lot before he changes his mind.

Chapter Eighteen

Jay

Kate hops off the back of my bike after I park in my building's small parking lot. It's quite the contrast to the brightly lit, expansive lot at her complex considering the burnt out lamps and beater cars. She pulls off her helmet, and I'm pleased to see a smile on her face. This girl is almost always smiling. I hope some of her positivity rubs off on me. Shit, if I'm being honest, that's not all I want her to rub on me.

I secure my bike to the lamppost I parked beside with a standard bicycle chain and padlock. It may not be the best way to prevent theft, but at least it deters thieves long enough for them to move on to easier targets. I've come out in the morning a few times to see it's been tampered with, but the bike is never gone, so it's working so far.

Taking Kate's hand in mine, I quickly pull her towards the building and up the stairs to the third floor. I'm practically dragging her, but I don't want her to get too good of a look around this hell hole, or for anyone to get a look at her. We get to my door, and the key jams in the stupid lock, as usual. After a few choice words and grunts, it finally turns and the door pops open. I quickly tug her inside and shut the door behind me, twisting the locks on the knob and deadbolt before engaging the chain lock.

I flip the light switch and watch as Kate takes in the small studio apartment I've called home the past few months. The entire thing is about the size of her living room, and it came fully furnished. At $400 a month, it was a steal for the area. The full-size bed has a brand new mattress on it, and the small loveseat has seen better days but it's comfortable and doesn't have too many stains, and the two-seater dinette set in the kitchen serves its purpose. Thankfully, I keep my place clean so that's one thing I don't have to be embarrassed about. The only thing, really.

It takes Kate all of thirty seconds to take in the entire apartment. "It's cute," she says, looking at me again. "But it's not you…at all. Why haven't you added any of your own personal touches?"

"I got the TV," I say, gesturing to the twenty inch flat screen resting on top of the used and abused dresser. The building offers free basic cable so I'd allowed myself the indulgence shortly after I moved in. I'd opted for a small television since there's a decent chance it'll end up being stolen anyway.

She frowns. "You need to add pictures or some color…or something."

I know exactly what she's seeing. The depressive nature of this entire place. I get it. That's just one of the many reasons I didn't want her here.

"This is just a stopping point for me," I tell her. It's the truth. I don't have long-term plans to be in this building. My goal is to save up enough money to afford a place in a better area. Maybe closer to Stanford. Although it would be farther from work, I'd do it for Kate. To be close to her so maybe we could see each other more than just once in a while. My schedule is pretty open, but between work and her school responsibilities, Kate is always busy. It makes it hard to spend time together, and if we're going to make a go of this, time together is important. We need to do all that couple stuff chicks read about in romance books and watch in chick flicks.

"A stopping point?" She's adorable when she's confused. Her nose scrunches up, and I just want to kiss it.

"Yeah," I say, stepping close to her and putting my hands on her hips. I smirk when her breath hitches. "It's just a place for me to eat and sleep until I can afford something better. It's not permanent."

“So are you planning to stay in California? Or go back home?”

“I’m staying,” I tell her, taking a step closer.

“Promise?” she asks quietly, leaning into me.

“I promise.”

Her smile is huge, but I barely see it before she’s lifting on the tips of her toes and kissing me. Her tongue slips into my mouth, and I caress it with mine. She tastes sweet, like honey and whatever foo-foo drink she was sipping at the club. She wraps her arms around my shoulders and I tighten mine on her waist. If we’re not careful, I’m going to end up tossing her on my bed and forgetting all the reasons that’s a bad idea.

When we finally break apart, we’re both breathless.

“Bathroom,” she says, and I point her to the door. Yep, no frills here at all, unless you count the fire escape which I personally think is a hazard all in itself.

I grab a bottle of water from the fridge and try to get my shit together while she’s out of the room. What am I supposed to do with her tonight? And dammit, how am I gonna sleep with her in my bed? Even if I sleep on the couch, I’m going to know she’s there. Plus, my sheets will smell like her…sweet like strawberries and cream. I run my hands down my face, this was such a bad idea.

"Everything okay?" she asks, startling me. I hadn't even heard the toilet flush. That's what I get for being trapped inside my head.

"Yeah, I was just thinking there isn't much to do here. I've got basic cable but no movies or anything. Plus it's late so there's most likely only infomercials on, or reruns of bad dramedies. I don't have any games…not even a deck of cards."

She steps over to me and sets her hand on my arm, and I instantly shut up. "Calm down. We don't have to do anything." She smiles, and I relax. "Like you said, it's late. We can just go to sleep."

I nod. Good idea. Sleep. Where I can think about her in my bed. G-R-E-A-T.

I put my unfinished water back in the fridge and realize I'm a terrible host. "I'm so sorry. Would you like something to drink?"

"I'm all right. But I could use something to sleep in," she says, gesturing to her skintight jeans. "Unless you don't mind me sleeping in my panties," she brings her hands to the button of her jeans.

I freeze. I'm sure I probably look like a deer caught in headlights.

Kate laughs. "I'm kidding. Jeez, you're so tense. Relax, Jay."

I exhale. She's going to kill me. "I can grab you a t-shirt and boxers?"

"That'd be great." She walks over to the couch and sits down, making quick work of her shoes...some sort of strappy sandal, just like the ones she was wearing the first day I met her. Yeah, I remember that shit. I remember everything about that day.

I grab a pair of boxers and the biggest t-shirt I have out of a drawer, hoping like hell it covers most of her. If I have to peek at skin like I did that night at her apartment when we watched *Halloween*, I might not make it. My will power was pretty much shot the moment she'd said "panties."

"Here you go," I say, handing her the clothes.

"Thanks," she says, taking them from me. "Do you have an extra toothbrush?"

"Under the sink," I tell her, and she thanks me before heading to the bathroom.

I watch her walk away and then grab a pair of sleep shorts and another pair of clean boxers out of the dresser. When she's finished in the bathroom, I go in to change and brush my teeth. When I come out, she's sitting on the couch, twisting her hands and looking nervous.

"What's the matter?"

She jumps at the sound of my voice and laughs awkwardly. "It's nothing."

I sit down next to her and take her hand. "It's something...what?"

She takes a deep breath. "This is going to sound totally stupid," she mumbles. "I've never spent the night with a guy before."

My eyebrows shoot up. "Really?" I know she's not a virgin, she'd told me that in one of our late night conversations, so it surprises me that not one of the guys she slept with actually slept with her.

"Dorms, roommates..." she says with a shrug, as if that explains it all. I guess it does. She hasn't exactly had a lot of freedom.

"Well, this will be a first for both of us then. I haven't had a sleepover either," I say with a smile, playfully bumping her shoulder with mine. She gives me a genuine smile then, and I stand up, reaching my hand out to her. She places her small hand in mine, and I tug her up to her feet. "Come on, you sleep on the inside."

She climbs across the bed, and I try not to look at her ass. I *try*, but I fail.

"Hey! Eyes up here," she says. I look up and she watching me over her shoulder, a knowing smirk on her face. Damn, she's sexy.

"Sorry," I grin. I'm not sorry. Not at all.

"Right," she says with a laugh, laying down and pulling the sheet over her body. I frown once my eye candy is concealed. "Come on, stud."

"Stud?" I ask as I walk over to the switch and turn the light off.

"Yeah...you have to know you're a stud."

"I don't know," I say, settling in beside her. We're each laying on our sides facing one another. "Tell me more."

She laughs and shoves me. "You're so bad."

"And you love it," I say, grabbing her hands before she pulls them away.

Her eyes meet mine, and in the dark, I can just barely see their twinkle. "I do...I do love it."

Chapter Nineteen

Kate

Lying beside Jay is intense. Lying beside Jay in his bed is even more intense. Lying beside Jay in his bed while he stares into my eyes is off the charts.

"You love that I'm bad?" he asks. He's still holding both my hands with one of his and it's driving me crazy because I *really* want to trace the tattoos on his body with my fingers...and my tongue.

"I love everything about you," I confess quietly. "And you're not *that* bad. Just misunderstood."

You know those moments...the ones where you can actually feel everything change in an instant? Sometimes they're good moments...sometimes they're bad. Nevertheless, they're a tipping point. A start of something new and different.

The first time I remember having one of those moments in a good way—probably the only time, too—was the day I was broke down on the side of the highway and suddenly looked into the most amazing eyes I'd ever seen. That moment had started Jay and me on the path of our rocky friendship. Our journey has been full of ups and downs, and it has had its fair share of distance and hostility—on his part, not mine—but look at us now. Here. Together. In bed.

Which brings me to the second time I've had one of those moments. Right now.

This is one of those moments.

Hell, this is *the* moment.

His eyes say so much more than his words, and that thought alone brings me so much comfort because I can finally see what he's thinking and feeling. His eyes tell me he cares, but that he's scared. Scared of what he's feeling, scared of hurting me, scared of the present and the future and the past. Especially the past. He's scared that he's not enough...that I'm too good. That he's too bad.

Well...challenge accepted.

I take a deep breath, trying to psych myself up—so grateful he had that extra toothbrush—and go all in. Pulling my hands loose, I raise myself up on my left elbow and gently rest my right hand on his cheek. I gaze into his eyes, the perfect silver orbs, then lean in and press my lips to his.

He's frozen for a moment, but only for a moment, before he kisses me back. He licks the seam of my mouth, and I open for him, loving the minty way he tastes. He's all in, too. He rolls onto his back, pulling me with him so I'm lying with my upper body draped over his. With my kisses, I tell him that he *is* good enough. I tell him not to be scared of anything...not of me, not of right now, not of tomorrow, and definitely not of yesterday.

I feel the moment when his walls fall down. He flips us over so I'm on my back and he's hovering over me. He's still kissing me, only now the delicious pressure of his hard-on is pressing straight against my center. I wrap my legs tightly around his waist and my arms around his shoulders, not wanting to let go. Ever.

He groans as I rock my hips against him, wanting to feel every last bit of friction. His arms are bent at the elbow, holding his upper body up, and his hands are fisted beside my head as if he's holding on by one last thread. I want to *snap* that thread.

I run my hands down his back and palm his ass. I can feel the tautness of the muscle through his thin pajama shorts. I squeeze, and he thrusts against me. I moan at the contact and continue to rock against him, using my grip on his ass as leverage and willing that little thread of resistance to snap.

It does. Oh, finally it does.

Jay sets himself upright, kneeling between my legs. He takes hold of my wrists in each hand and comes back down on top of me, holding my wrists above my head. I feel so open, so vulnerable lying here before him. I love it.

He takes my mouth in a seething kiss and presses his erection against me.

"Please, Jay," I beg against his mouth.

"Please what?" he teases, running the tip of his tongue from the corner of my mouth, down to my jaw, then tracing my jawline up to my earlobe. When he reaches his destination, he nibbles and I whimper with need.

"Make love to me," I gasp, feeling like I'm about ready to explode from the feel of him pressed against me.

He faces me again and looks into my eyes, his reflecting the same vulnerability as mine. "I've never done that before," he says softly, and I know he's referring to my request to make love. Not sex in general. We both have pasts.

"Neither have I," I tell him honestly.

He lets go of my wrists, and his hands frame my face as though I'm the most precious thing to him...maybe I am. "Kate..."

I put my finger to his lips, not wanting him to start speaking of all the ways this is not a good idea. This is the best freaking idea I've ever had, and I'm not letting him talk himself out of it. This is good and right and perfect, and I won't let him ruin it by professing all the reasons he thinks he's bad news. Because he's not bad news. He's not. He's perfect, and he's mine and I want this. So I tell him exactly that.

"I'm not perfect, Kate...far from it," he responds with a loathsome tone.

"If you keep talking about my man that way, I'll have to kick your ass," I say, nipping at his full bottom lip with my teeth and letting it go with a pop.

"Your man, huh?"

"Was there ever a doubt?"

His eyes soften, and he shakes his head. "I don't know what I did to deserve you, Sunshine."

My heart warms at the endearment. "You were just yourself, Jay. That's all I ever want you to be."

He presses his lips to mine again, effectively ending our conversation. We slowly strip off one another's clothes, taking time to admire every piece of each other with touches and kisses. Then finally, when there's nothing left between us, he makes love to me.

Twice.

***

Last night was amazing.

We'd played and talked until the wee hours of the morning, and then I fell asleep in his arms. When we'd woken up some time in the early afternoon, I'd finally gotten to trace those tattoos of his and he told me about each and every one of them. He has almost complete sleeves on each arm and more on his chest and back. Some are colorful, some are just black, but they all mean something to him.

My favorite is his most recent. It's an artistically drawn sun on his arm, just below his shoulder. He'd confessed that it reminds him of me...because I'm his light. He got it when he'd first arrived in California. The fact he got a tattoo to remind him of me should have freaked me out, but it didn't. The sentiment brought tears to my eyes, and I knew right then and there that I was falling in love with him. Not that I can tell him that, though. It would probably send him running. Which is completely ridiculous since he permanently marked himself with a symbol of me. If that doesn't indicate he's in deep, I'm not quite sure what else will. I guess I'll just have to wait for him to catch on.

We make love one more time before he takes me to a late lunch and then drops me off at home. I have a shift at Five tonight, so I have to step off my cloud and rejoin reality. Smiling to myself at the memory of the soft kisses we'd shared before he finally rode off, I let myself into the apartment.

The lights are out inside the apartment, which is odd since I saw Casey's car in the parking lot. It's also very quiet. I find it hard to believe Casey and Decker can be that quiet. I hope they didn't get into another fight. They really need to figure their shit out. They're so perfect for each other it's annoying. I briefly consider that they might actually be getting along—really well, if you know what I mean—but even that would produce a sound or two. I feel the heat in my cheeks as I think about the sounds that must have been coming from Jay's apartment last night.

I set my things down on the table in the entryway and head down the hall, desperate for a shower. As much as I hate to wash the evening and morning and afternoon off of me, I can't exactly show up to work looking like I was ridden hard and put away wet. Even though I *so* was. I giggle at the dirty thought.

I start the shower and while it heats up—I like lots of steam—I decide to check on Casey. I guess she and Decker could have walked to the café or taken a cab somewhere, but I doubt it. And it's too late—or too early—for them to be asleep. I knock on the door and there's no answer. I try the knob, and it's locked. An uneasy feeling creeps over me.

Not again. Please, not again.

I bang on the door, hoping to wake Casey up if she's sleeping. *If* she's sleeping. No. I'm not going to think that way. "Casey!" I call out, banging on the door again. "Casey, open up!"

Nothing. Just utter stillness.

I go into my bedroom and open the top drawer of my nightstand. Somewhere in here is one of those stupid little flat-head pin keys that'll open Casey's door. *Where is it?* Ah-ha! Found it. I quickly go back to Casey's door and unlock it.

What happens next is another one of those moments. Only this one is bad. Very, very bad.

Casey's lying on her bed, curled around her pillow. Her skin is pale and her lips have a bluish hue. I'm frozen in shock in the doorway for a moment, but only for a moment because my instincts kick in. After all, this isn't the first time this has happened.

To me...or to Casey...

I check for a pulse...it's faint, but it's there. I roll her onto her back and check her airway. Clear. I begin CPR.

My movements are mechanical. Clinical. It's almost as though I'm outside of myself, looking in. I'm terrified, but I'm not. I want to cry, but I can't.

I spot Casey's phone on the nightstand as I'm doing my compressions and quickly grab it, telling Siri to call 911. She complies and pretty soon, I have a dispatcher on the line. I'm giving her directions through the speakerphone while pounding on my best friend's chest.

She is *not* going to die on me.

Chapter Twenty

Jay

I probably broke at least ten traffic laws rushing to the hospital to be with Kate. Quite honestly, her call scared the shit out of me. Kate's a passionate person. She speaks with liveliness and emotion, no matter the subject. So when she'd called to say she was at the hospital with Casey and that it didn't look good—all in a robotic, monotone voice—I panicked. I freaked the fuck out. What the hell had happened?

I knew a little about Casey's condition, but not much. Kate didn't feel right disclosing too much of her roommate's personal business. I couldn't blame her for that. I hadn't realized that whatever was up with her had the potential to land her in the hospital, though.

I spot Kate almost immediately as I enter the emergency room. She's sitting in the waiting area, stiff and stoic, staring into space. It's not until I'm directly in front of her that she registers my presence. I crouch down in front of her and place my hands on her knees. She makes eye contact, but it's like she's not even there. Her brown eyes are flat…empty.

"I did CPR. She almost died in the ambulance. I called her mother. She's flying out. I don't know where Decker is. He wasn't at the apartment."

I have no idea what to say. I'm not even sure how to process what she's just told me. She had to perform CPR on Casey? I can't imagine what that must have been like. And Casey almost died? Holy shit. I can't think of a single thing to say that might make this situation even an ounce better for her.

And she still has that tone…lifeless and dull. It's as though she's reading from a script, like how I imagine a harried emergency room doctor would inform the fiftieth family of the night of their loved one's condition. That's so *not* the Kate I know. She's not this shell of a person before me.

I sit down beside her without saying anything and take her hand in mine. She lets me, and I take some selfish comfort in that. At least I know she's still in there somewhere. And so we wait. We wait, we wait, and we wait. Eventually the doctor comes out to speak with us—well, to speak with Kate as she is listed in Casey's medical records as her next of kin since Casey's parents are so far away.

The doctor says a lot of things I don't understand, but Kate seems to understand with perfect clarity. I do pick up on some key words. Casey's condition is stable, but she's still unconscious. He tells us we can go see her as soon as they settle her into a room.

About an hour later, we're taken to Casey's room by a nurse. She asks us to notify someone at the nurses' station when Casey wakes up. They seem optimistic that she will wake up soon. That's a good thing. As soon as the nurse exits the room, Kate looks at her roommate and promptly...finally...bursts into tears. I take her in my arms and hold her while she weeps, eventually moving us to an armchair in the corner of the small room. Kate cries herself to sleep right there in my lap.

***

"Did you see that?" Kate asks me about thirty minutes later. Turns out, all my girl needed was a quick power nap. She'd slept for about twenty minutes and woke up a different person. She's still sad, but there's a little more light in her eyes. She'd needed that cry and the nap.

"See what?" I ask.

"She just moved her foot," Kate says, pointing to Casey's leg.

"Oh yeah?"

"There it went again! And her fingers just twitched." Kate hops off my lap and steps towards the bed. "I think she's starting to wake up."

I get up, taking a minute to stretch, then stand beside Kate. "Should I get the nurse?"

"Let's wait a minute."

Casey's eyes flutter a little, then her right eye opens for a moment. She quickly closes it.

"Casey?" Kate says, walking around to the side of the bed to take Casey's hand. "If you can hear me, squeeze my hand." Kate smiles, so Casey must have responded. "She's responsive."

"I'll go get the doctor," I tell Kate. I step over and give her a kiss on her temple, but her eyes don't leave her roommate. I quietly let myself out of the room and make my way down to the nurses' station, which, of course, is empty. It takes me several minutes to find someone who can page Casey's doctor.

Chapter Twenty-One

Kate

"You scared the hell out of me, Casey Evans," I hiss as soon as the door closes behind Jay.

"Sorry," she responds in a husky whisper. I'm sure her throat is dry. I look around for a pitcher of water but there isn't one. I'll have to remember to tell the nurse to bring one in.

"Sorry isn't going to cut it."

I'm well aware that I shouldn't be scolding my best friend while she's barely coherent in a hospital bed, but I'm at the end of my rope. I'm close...so close...to losing it, she has no idea. Now that I've had time to reflect on the day's events, I can finally recall the terror I'd felt when I let myself into her bedroom and found her unresponsive. The horrifying thoughts of "Not again, this can't be happening again!" and the sheer disappointment that I'd even had that thought in the first place.

Casey should have taken better care of herself than this, but she hasn't. She's given up. You'd think that after her father passed away and she saw what that did to her mom, she'd reconsider her treatment options. You'd think that she'd find a will to live...to make herself better. If not for the people who love her, than at least for herself. She's got so much potential. And she's throwing it all away. I don't know how she can live with her decisions because I'm pretty sure I can't anymore.

"What happened?"

"You had a cardiac episode." Casey flinches. "You nearly arrested in the ambulance on the way to the hospital."

"Decker?"

I laugh, now she's worried about Decker? "You're just lucky he wasn't around."

"I kicked him out," she whispers.

"You what?" I can't believe my ears. She kicked Decker out? That guy flew across the country to be with her and she kicks him out? At least she has the decency to look upset...remorseful even.

"I'm sorry," Casey says.

"For what, exactly? For almost dying in our apartment? Not for the first time, I might add. For scaring the shit out of me? Again, not for the first time." I'm counting her offenses off on my fingers as I list them. "For not telling the guy you are *so* obviously in love with that you have a heart condition that you refuse to seek help for? Which one is it, Casey? What exactly are you sorry for?"

Casey closes her eyes—while I recognize that this isn't the time or the place for this conversation, it's long overdue. Casey needs some tough love. It's about time she starts thinking about things on a larger level. Her decisions effect everyone, not just her.

"For everything," she says finally. "All of that. I'm sorry for all of it."

I take Casey's hand, and the tears that were building behind my lids finally break through.

"I love you, Casey. You know that. You're my best friend. I've stood by you through so much, and you've stood by me, too. But I can't do this anymore. I can't watch you self-destruct. Coming home this afternoon and not being able to wake you up? You were starting to turn *blue*. I thought it was the end. The *end* end. I was so scared."

Casey opens her eyes and takes in my tear-soaked face. "I'm sorry, Kate."

"Sorry isn't good enough, Casey!" I close my eyes tight, immediately sorry for snapping but unable to hold back my frustration.

"Then what *do* you want me to say?" she snaps back. At least she's still got some of her feistiness. Makes me feel a little less bad about what I'm about to do.

"Nothing! I don't want you to *say* anything. I want you to *do*!"

"Well, that's not going to happen," my stubborn roommate says quietly.

I shake my head. "I can't sit by and watch you kill yourself any longer."

Casey rolls her eyes—yes, she has the nerve to roll her eyes—minimizing my concern for her and my feelings all in one gesture. "That's a bit dramatic, don't you think?"

"No, I don't think it is."

"I'm not killing myself, Kate. My body is doing a damn good job of that on its own."

"You're refusing treatment," I say, crossing my arms.

"I take my medication," she bites back.

"You're prolonging your life, Casey. You're not saving it." God, can't she see it? Can't she see what she's doing to herself and to those who care about her?

"It's my decision to make!" Casey yells, causing the heart monitor to beep excitedly. I take a step back. I shouldn't have done this right now, but it's too late.

"You're right, Casey. It is your decision. And it's my decision not to be a part of it anymore." It's like the floodgates have broken, there's no holding back the tears now as they drip down my cheeks. I can taste their saltiness on my lips.

"What are you saying?" she whispers, a few tears escaping her eyes now.

"I'm saying I can't sit back and wait with you for you to die anymore. I understand that I don't know what's it's like to be you, to be diagnosed with a potentially terminal disease. But Casey, you have options. This doesn't have to be a dead end street for you. There are roads where you can turn off, and you won't explore them...you won't even slow the car down. You're twenty-one years old, and you've given up on yourself."

"Kate, we've talked about this—"

"No, we haven't talked about this," I insist adamantly. "The doctor laid it all out for you and you chose. And you chose poorly. I don't know what made you give up on life, Casey. But I can't handle it anymore. I may be strong, but I'm not that strong. I can't watch my best friend fall apart this way when there is a solution. The Casey I met freshman year was a fighter. Where did she go?"

I hear the door open behind me and look over to see Jay walk in. I wipe my eyes, but it's no use. The tears keep coming.

Giving up on your best friend isn't easy. Even if it's with both of your best interests at heart.

Chapter Twenty-Two

Jay

When I return to the room, I'm not quite sure what I've walked in on. Kate and Casey both have tears streaming down their faces and both look incredibly sad.

"The doctor will be here in a minute," I tell them.

Kate nods and offers me a small smile. She then steps closer to Casey's bedside and kisses her forehead. "I love you, Casey. Please…take care of yourself."

Casey closes her eyes and more tears stream down her cheeks. I still have no idea what the hell's going on…but that almost sounded like a goodbye. I look questioningly at Kate and she just shakes her head and hastily leaves the room. I look back at Casey; her eyes are still closed, and her face is still wet with tears. Not knowing what else to do, I turn and follow Kate out.

Kate stops by the nurses' station on the way out and asks them to bring Casey some water. She's quiet on the ride home. I left my bike in the hospital parking garage, choosing to worry about it later, so I could drive Kate back to her apartment in her car. I don't want to push her to talk about what happened between her and Casey; I know she'll talk when she's ready, but I'm really confused as to why she isn't elated her friend is awake and seemingly well.

We get to her apartment and—unfortunately—Decker's waiting outside the apartment when we arrive, so Kate has the pleasure of explaining Casey's situation to him. The guy is absolutely wrecked. It's obvious that his love for Casey goes way beyond friendship. He just caves in on himself. I've never seen anyone look more destroyed than Decker does in this moment.

It's hard seeing the two of them look so defeated, and I finally get a sense of the strain Casey's health has put on Kate. I learn that this isn't even the first time this has happened. I can't imagine Kate living in regular fear that one day she may wake up or come home and Casey might be unconscious...or worse. It takes a special person to take on that kind of responsibility, and Kate is definitely special. I'm not sure I could live like that. I'm not sure I could stand the constant anxiety.

Kate completely breaks down while telling Decker Casey's story. She lets me hold her, and, again, I find myself feeling selfishly grateful. That little allowance makes me feel like I'm doing something right in the middle of all this wrong. It's the first time all evening I haven't felt utterly useless. My Sunshine, the light of my life, is breaking. And I'm powerless to stop it. It's the most helpless feeling I've ever had. And that's saying something.

After a while, a dejected Decker heads off to the hospital with a spare key to the apartment in case Casey's mom needs a place to sleep, and Kate and I are left alone. I hate that she had to tell Decker about Casey's heart condition. It should have been Casey. She shouldn't have kept it from him. For him to have found out like that from someone he barely knows is just wrong. If it were Kate keeping something like that from me...I just don't know what I'd do.

Kate and I sit silently on the couch. She's looking more alert than she has all night, but she's still absent. Her mind is still running on all cylinders.

Her hands are curled up on her lap, and I gently place one of mine on top and squeeze. "You okay?"

She looks up at me, her eyes tired and sad. "I don't really think I want to be here," she says, timidly looking around the apartment as if she's waiting for something to jump out at her. "Can we go to your place?"

I don't want to take her back to my place, but I can tell she's desperate to be anywhere but here. I nod in agreement and stand, pulling her up with me. I wrap her in my arms and hold on tight. "I'm so sorry about all this, Sunshine."

She sniffles against my chest and wraps her arms around my back, holding me like she'll never let go. Deep sobs make her small body shudder, and I kiss the top of her head.

"Shh...it's okay, baby," I soothe, running my fingers through her hair. She seems to like it when I do that.

She sniffs and takes a step back, frowning at the tearstains on my shirt. "I'm so sorry," she says. Her apology is unnecessary. I'd do anything for her, a few tears on my shirt don't bother me one bit.

"It'll dry," I tell her with a small smile.

"I'm just going to grab some clothes."

I nod and watch as she walks off. She's so tough and independent. If anyone can go through what she's gone through today and make it out on top, Kate can. She's the strongest person I know. I smile at her when she returns to the living room, and she blushes. Pink looks good on her cheeks.

"Do you mind if we swing by the hospital on the way...so I can grab my bike? If you're not okay to drive...or if you don't want to go back there, I understand. I can get Tom or Johnny to pick it up for me." I know I'm babbling, but I don't want her to feel any pressure. My bike can stay in hospital parking for a week, I don't care.

"I don't mind. I'm okay to drive." She smiles a genuine smile, and I relax.

"Let's go then," I say, taking the small pink duffel bag from her hand and tossing it over my shoulder. The sight makes Kate giggle. I roll my eyes playfully and take her hand, pulling her out the door.

Chapter Twenty-Three

Kate

An hour later we're lying on our sides in Jay's bed again, my back to his front and his arms holding me tight. It feels so different from the last time we were in this position, less than 24 hours ago, yet I feel so safe and adored. I'm not sure I'll ever be able to fall asleep a different way.

"Tell me more about your family," I ask, wanting to think about anything but Casey, and I feel his body stiffen in response.

Most of our conversations, verbal and written, have revolved around me and what's going on in my life. My friends, my family, my problems. Very little has been about Jay. I know he has a brother, Mac, and I know both he and his brother don't have contact with their parents, but I don't know why. Judging by his silence, the lack of information he's shared about his family has been intentional.

"You sure you want to talk about me? You went through a lot today. Don't you want to talk about what happened?"

That's the last thing I want to do. I'm aware bottling up my emotions isn't healthy, but I'm not sure I'm ready to relive today's events. From finding Casey to saying goodbye. I just can't do it. Not tonight.

"No, I want to know more about you."

"What do you want to know?" he asks after an awkward silence, the tension clear in his voice.

I'm about to tell him to tell me whatever he wants to, but then he wouldn't tell me anything, and I feel like I *need* to know something. "Do you know where your parents are?"

He lets out a breath against my neck. "Last Mac heard they were living somewhere in West Columbia."

"They're still together?"

I feel rather than see him shrug his shoulders. "I don't know. I didn't ask, he didn't tell."

"When's the last time you spoke to them?"

"When I was sixteen."

"That's when you went to live with Mac?"

"Yeah. They were both big into drugs then. The last night I saw them they were having a party in the trailer we rented. Someone called the cops. They got busted for drugs. Mac was getting ready to graduate from the police academy and had an apartment. I guess I got lucky that he wanted me so I didn't end up in foster care."

Granted, my parents were not going to win any parenting awards in their lifetimes, but I still couldn't imagine not speaking to them for years. They're my parents, and I love them, and I think, in their own way, they love me, too. I can't imagine what it must have been like for Jay, and even Mac, having parents who couldn't have cared less about them. Parents who would put their kids' lives in danger like that.

"Why wouldn't he have wanted you?" I ask.

"He was twenty-two years old, what twenty-two year old guy wants to take in his worthless, little brother?"

"Mac," I answer matter-of-factly. "And don't call yourself worthless. You're not worthless."

"I grew up being told I was worthless every damn day. It's kind of hard to not believe it."

"Well, your parents are fools for thinking that. You're worth something Jason Spencer. You're worth a lot."

He gets quiet, and I don't think he's going to say anything further on the subject, but then he surprises me by speaking again. "I never thanked him, you know? I was an ungrateful little shit most of the time, rebelling against every authority figure I could...maybe because I couldn't take out my frustrations on my own parents. He put up with it and set me straight though."

"And you turned into a pretty awesome guy despite it all."

He lets out a mocking laugh. "Right."

I roll over so I'm facing him, looking into his gray eyes. "You are an awesome guy, Jay. You're decent and hardworking. You're caring and smart and funny and sweet and sexy."

The side of his mouth quirks up. "You think I'm sexy?"

I laugh, of course, that's what he got from all that. "The sexiest."

I lean in to give him a chaste kiss on the lips, but he doesn't want any of that. He presses his lips against mine with such fervor that I can't help but moan at the contact. He can't hide his need for me...his want...he rolls us over so I'm on my back, and he's on top of me, still kissing me deeply.

Kissing Jay is something else...like a magic that sends sparks flying throughout every part of my body. It's the best therapy for the emotional and stressful day I've had.

We roll around his bed, making out like a couple teenagers for what seems like hours before finally falling into an exhausted and restful sleep.

Yep...not sure I'll ever be able to fall asleep without this particular nightly ritual again.

Chapter Twenty-Four

Jay

The bright sun shining through the cracks in the blinds eventually wakes me up, and I'm so glad it does. Lying beside me is the most beautiful girl in the world, and I don't want to miss a minute of this. The way the sunlight reflects off her golden hair makes it look like she's got a halo hovering perfectly over her head. She's so gorgeous. Her soft skin is almost completely bare, save for the tiny pajamas she's wearing. I'm starting to like her sleepwear.

As much as I'd like to stay in bed with her all morning—again—I know she hasn't eaten since our late lunch yesterday, so I'm going to make her breakfast. After I dropped her off yesterday, I'd gone to the grocery store to get milk, eggs, sausage, and some other stuff. In fact, I'd just finished unloading the groceries when I got her phone call.

I shake my head. I can't believe that was only yesterday. I feel like the entire evening aged me. I'm not sure I'd ever been so scared and freaked out in my life. I didn't know what to do with Kate in that state, and I'm so glad she seemed to start to come back as the evening wore on. When we were in bed last night, she was almost completely back to her old self. Almost. But I'd noticed how the light in her eyes was still a bit dim before we finally succumbed to sleep.

Not that I can blame her. I'll give her all the time she needs to cope with what went down yesterday, though I'm hoping she'll confide in me about what she and Casey talked about when I'd left the room. I thought Casey waking up would have brought Kate back to life, but it didn't. In fact, it seemed to have made her sadder.

I'm not sure I'll ever understand women.

I've just cracked eggs into the frying pan when I feel her hands slide around my middle. I drop the cracked shells on the now empty sausage tray and put my hands on top of hers. I could get used to this.

"Good morning," she says, her voice still husky with sleep...and so incredibly sexy that I'm glad she's behind me and not in front of me, or she'd know just how sexy I think she is.

"Good morning."

"To what do I owe this pleasure?" she asks. "It smells so good."

"Who says it's for you?" I ask, releasing her hands to grab the spatula.

She gives my abs a hard pat. "Not funny. I'm starved." On cue, her stomach growls, and I laugh. "That's so embarrassing," she says, releasing me.

"I was making you breakfast in bed," I tell her, looking over my shoulder. Damn. She's sexy as hell with bed head and sleep hooded eyes.

"Well, then...I'd better get back in bed," she winks.

I groan, then turn back to the stove, subtly adjusting myself as I hear her settling back in. I finish up the eggs and sausage, then set them all on one plate. I pour a tall glass of milk, grab a fork, and balance it all as I walk to the bed.

"I could have helped," she offers as she takes the plate from me. I set the milk down on the nightstand and get in bed beside her. "What are you eating?" she asks with a smirk.

"We're sharing," I tell her as I fork up some eggs and feed them to her.

"Mmm, this is so good."

"They're just eggs."

"They're not *just* eggs. They're eggs that *you* made for *me*."

Her smile undoes me, and I feel something deep in my chest. Is it love? I don't know. I don't know if I'm capable of that kind of emotion. It's not like I've got the best role models in that department. Then again, Kate doesn't exactly have the best role models for love either.

Maybe we can learn together.

"What do you want to do today?" I ask her once we clear the plate.

"You don't have to work?"

"Nah, I'm off." I don't tell her that I'd called Leroy yesterday and taken today off so I could be with her. Leroy had been a little pissed off, but since I'm a good employee and never miss work, he let me have the day.

She swallows a sip of milk and looks at me with a mischievous sparkle in her eyes and Cheshire cat grin on her face. "I want to get a tattoo!"

I almost choke on my own sip of milk. "What?"

"I want to get a tattoo," she repeats.

"I don't think that's a good idea," I tell her.

"Why not?" she frowns.

"They're permanent, Kate."

Her frown deepens along with the crease in between her eyebrows. “Duh.”

“I just don’t think it’s something you should jump into.”

“Who says I’m jumping into anything?” she asks defiantly, crossing her arms over her ample breasts.

“You’ve never mentioned a tattoo before, Sunshine. I just think you should take some time to think about it.”

She groans and throws herself back on the bed. “I’m so sick of *thinking* about things. I just want to *do* things!”

Where is this coming from? I admit that she and I haven’t spent a whole lot of time together, but I feel like I do know her, especially through our conversations and her letters. Kate is a very careful, calculated, thorough person. She thinks things through. She doesn’t just do them.

“What’s going on, Kate? Talk to me,” I place the cup and plate on the nightstand and lie beside her on the bed and pull her towards me.

“I feel like I haven’t really been living, Jay. I’m predictable. I go through the motions and do everything that’s expected of me. My resume is exceptional with steady employment, numerous volunteer activities, and excellent academics, but when it comes to having fun and living life to its fullest…it’s blank.”

She looks at me with those dark, sad eyes…begging me to understand. And I do. Finally, I do. The incident with Casey has rocked her world. She understands the fragility of life now more than ever before and wants to seize the day.

I let out a sigh and smile at my girl. “As long as you don’t get ‘YOLO’ tattooed on your ass, I’ll support your decision.” She laughs loudly and gives me a big, sloppy kiss on the cheek. I fight the urge to wipe off my face because I simply can’t break this moment. She finally looks happy, free. “So what are you gonna get?” I ask, nuzzling her neck.

“Well, you nixed my only idea so I’ve got to start thinking about it all over again.”

This time I laugh. “Seriously?”

“No, not seriously. But you’re right. A tattoo is permanent, so I need to think about it some more. I still want one, but maybe that’s not what we need to do today.”

I kiss her lips. She’s practical even when she tries to rebel. It’s adorable. “So what’s on the agenda then, rebel?”

She grins at that. “Well…I’ve got to call my boss. I think I need a couple days off.” I nod in agreement. I think she could use a few mental health days. Hopefully he’ll be understanding. “Then I’m all yours.”

“I like the sound of that,” I say, then I lean in to kiss her neck.

“Stop that,” she says, giggling as she slaps my back. “Jay!”

“Okay, okay,” I say, pulling away. “Go do your thing. I’ll be right here waiting for you.”

She softly smiles at me, and I hope she knows that I don’t just mean right now...that I mean I’ll always be right here waiting for her. As long as she’ll have me.

I’m starting to hope that it’s forever.

Chapter Twenty-Five

Kate

After running out to the store to get a DVD player—my treat—and then to a Red Box to get a few DVDs, Jay and I spend the rest of the morning relaxing in bed and watching movies. We order takeout from a nearby Chinese restaurant and eat lunch at Jay's tiny kitchen table.

I'd spoken to my boss. He was understanding of the situation and gave me an entire week off. Thankfully, I'm in between semesters so I don't have to worry about classes; however, I did contact the tutoring center on campus and ask not to be put on the schedule. I don't tutor often, but occasionally if there's a student who needs assistance with a subject I'm particularly good in, they'll schedule me.

"Do you want to go see Casey today?" Jay asks, and my entire body tenses.

I set down my chop sticks and shake my head. Hopefully, he'll leave it alone. I know I'll need to go see Casey again and apologize for being an emotional bitch, but I'm not ready yet. Plus, she needs to work this stuff out with Decker. They need some time alone together. And there's always the chance she might not even want to talk to me.

"Everything okay with the two of you? Things seemed kind of tense when I walked in the room last night."

So much for hoping he'll leave it alone. I let out a sigh and try to decide what to tell him. I owe him some explanation after the condition he saw me in yesterday.

"Living with Casey is...a challenge. I love her; she's my best friend, but I want to slap the shit out of her at the same time. I said some things to her last night...things I probably—no, definitely—shouldn't have said given the circumstances, but I needed to get them off my chest, and I needed her to realize that she can't keep doing this to herself and the people who love her."

"What's she doing?"

I sigh. "She's giving up. And I hate her for it. And I hate that I hate her for it. It's her life...I know that...but I don't want my best friend to die."

Jay nods sympathetically. "Tough love?" he asks.

"Something like that," I mumble.

"I know a little bit about that. It never really seems like the right time or place when you're on the receiving end of tough love."

"Mac?" I ask.

"Yeah. I earned quite a few speeches from him. All necessary, too. Of course, I didn't realize it then. At the time, I was pissed off at him. I thought he was being an asshole. But, in retrospect, I understand where he was coming from...what he was saying. Just wish I'd realized it a little sooner."

Just like Casey hopefully will. I reach over the table and take his hand in mine, twining our fingers together. "Thank you."

"For what?"

"You always know the right things to say."

He squeezes my hand gently. "She'll come around."

"I hope so."

"She will. Who wouldn't want to have you in their life?"

My parents briefly flash into my mind, but I quickly push them out. I don't want them to taint this special moment with Jay.

Truthfully, I don't want them to taint any moment with him. I know if Jay and I get any more serious, he'll eventually have to meet them, but I hope we can push that off for as long as possible. I don't want to subject him to them and their judgmental ways.

"Where'd you go?" he asks, tearing me from my unwanted thoughts.

"Thinking about my parents," I tell him honestly.

He scowls. "They're crazy. You know that, right?"

I shrug. "They're my parents, Jay."

"I know, baby. And I think it's pretty amazing that you still care so much about what they think and want. I'm not going to disrespect that because it's the way you feel, but I just want you to know that regardless of what they say or do—or don't do...you're an amazing person. With or without them."

I smile. He really does know all the right things to say. "Thanks, Jay."

He smiles back. "Anytime, Sunshine."

***

"What do you want to be when you grow up?" I ask Jay later that night. We'd just made love, and I'm lying across his body while he runs his fingers through my hair.

"I'd love to open my own repair shop."

"Cars or bikes?"

"Either. Both. I don't know. I love bikes, but if I did cars, too, I'd have a larger market. Sean's got a motorcycle shop back home, and I bet he'd help me get one started somewhere."

"You'd be so good at it," I tell him through a yawn.

"What about you?" he asks me.

"You already know," I tell him.

"Teaching?" he asks.

I smile, pleased he remembers the conversation. "Yeah."

"So why not just go for it."

"I can't, Jay." We'd already talked about this, too.

"Because of your parents," he says flatly.

"They don't support that choice for me."

"But it's your choice," he argues.

I sigh. How do I make him understand? "Excelling at my studies is the only thing that's ever seemed to please my parents. It's the only thing that's ever even gotten me on their radar. If I go against their wishes...then what do I have?"

The room is silent as Jay processes what I've said. He probably thought the only thing holding me back was the funding. Sure, the financial support from my parents plays a huge role in my life. They pay for my education, my housing, and my car. They even give me an allowance for living expenses. I don't use all of it. Only what I need to survive. I'm not one of those college kids with the rich parents who blow through every dime their parents give them. I'm frugal. I work when I don't have to just so I can have my own money, separate from theirs, to do things I know they wouldn't approve of—like buying DVD players in the bad part of town or getting a tattoo.

So yeah, if I switched majors and decided to pursue a career in education, my parents would pull my funding. They wouldn't pay for college or housing. I'd get no allowance. They may let me keep my car, or they may take it away out of disappointment and spite. It would be difficult to start over, but not impossible. I could do it without their money...I could get loans and work. I wouldn't have to complete a full four years of college since I've already completed most of my gen. ed. requirements, so I wouldn't have to fully finance a degree. Hell, with my grades I could probably even get some scholarships. The possibilities were endless.

But if I did that, I'd lose what very little connection I have left with my parents. Their occasional visits when they're on the west coast for conferences or the rare phone call when I've done something to catch their attention. Even though they're usually harping on me for something negative or irrational, it's still attention. Without that, I wouldn't even be a blip on their radar. I guess part of me will always be that little girl seeking her parents' approval.

"How often do you see your mom and dad?"

"Maybe once or twice a year," I admit sadly.

"Talk to them?"

"Every couple months." *If that,* I think to myself.

Jay lifts my chin and looks into my eyes. "So how different would it really be?"

I roll off of him and sit up, tucking the sheet around me. "What are you saying?"

He sits up beside me and takes my hands in his. "I don't know. Probably nothing worth paying attention to...but this is the rest of your life you're talking about. You're not happy in med school. Sure, you can do it. You're a genius, you can do whatever you want to do. But if you're not happy...God, Kate. You need to do what makes you happy, or you're going to be miserable for the rest of your life. I don't want you to be miserable. You've got this light about you. I think I'd die if it ever went out."

Chapter Twenty-Six

Jay

Kate stares at me without saying anything for what feels like hours, when really a minute hasn't even passed. I'm afraid I've gone too far, said too much, when she finally puts me out of my misery and speaks.

"YOLO."

"What?" What the fuck is she YOLOing for? That term is freaking terrible.

She smiles her biggest smile at me, and I think maybe everything is going to be okay. "YOLO, Jay."

"Yeah. I'm not following."

"I only have one life to live, Jay. You're right. I don't want to be miserable. I don't want to be a doctor. I want to teach. I want to help others grow and develop to be the best they can be. Whether it's in math, science, literature, or French." She starts speaking in what I guess is French, and man, I've never heard anything so sexy.

I tackle her onto the bed, and she yelps. "Say that again," I demand, licking a line from her collarbone down to her breast.

"*Saviez-vous que je parle français?*"

"I have no idea what you just say, but it was sexy as hell."

"*Tu es sexy,*" she breathes.

I press my erection against her as I suck a nipple into my mouth, causing her to whimper. "Keep talking," I urge her.

"*Je crois que je suis en train de tomber amoureux avec toi.*"

"More," I say as I make my way further down her body.

"*Oh, mon Dieu! Ne vous arrêtez pas*!"

Fuck. I have no idea what the hell she's talking about, and I don't care. She could be reciting the phone book, but that hot little accent she uses when she speaks...I just want to flip her over, pull her ass into the air, and pound right into her.

But Kate deserves to be worshipped, so that's what I'm going to do. I lower myself between her legs and with one quick swipe of my tongue, she screams my name in a combination of surprise and ecstasy.

"Keep talking, Sunshine."

"*Qui se sent bien.*"

As I lick and suck at her sweet center, she continues to mutter things I don't understand in French until spasms start racking through her body, and she cries out my name. Her body shudders for several long moments, and I finally crawl back up her body and soundly kiss her on the mouth.

She looks deep into my eyes and says, "*Je ne crois pas ... Je sais.*"

"What?" I ask, still not knowing what she's saying.

She just shakes her head and lifts her head up to kiss me. I let it all go for now, knowing that she'll tell me in English when she wants me to hear it. Her head falls back on the pillow and she gives me a soft, satisfied smile.

I'm pretty sure I've just fallen for this girl.

***

"So were you serious about all that stuff last night?" I ask Kate over breakfast. I'm curious if it was all just pillow talk, or if she's serious about switching her major. It would be a huge change for her...an overhaul of her entire life, pretty much.

She tenses and looks at me with wide eyes for a moment, and then seems to relax as she smiles. Interesting. "Yeah, I think I am."

I reach across the table and take her hand. "I'm proud of you, Sunshine. You know I'll be there for you in any way that you need me to be."

"I do know that. Thank you."

"How are you going to break the news to your parents?"

She shrugs and pops another forkful of eggs in her mouth. "They'll be here in a few weeks. I guess I'll tell them then. It'll be better to do it in person. They'll actually have to listen to me and they'll *see* that I'm serious."

I nearly choke on my toast. Her parents are going to be here in a few weeks? The two most detached people I've ever had described to me. I hope she doesn't ask me to meet them.

"I'd love it if you'd be there with me," she says, flipping her hand over and threading her fingers with mine. "They're not going to take it well, and I could really use someone in my corner. I can't ask Casey right now..."

Fuck.

"Of course, I'll be there for you," I choke out after taking a healthy swig of orange juice to clear the toast that's suddenly too dry from my throat. Because despite how I feel about her awful parents, I would do anything for her, though she'd never know since my agreement just came out like I consented to a death sentence.

"It's not gonna be *that* bad," she laughs. "They'll barely pay any attention to you. It'll be the ideal 'meet the parents' scenario. They'll be so pissed at me that they won't have any time to criticize you."

"Way to make a guy feel special, babe," I shake my head with a smirk, letting her know I'm joking with her.

"It's just my parents have something to say about everyone. I had a boyfriend sophomore year, Paul..."

I sort of tune her out as she talks about her old boyfriend. I know she's not a virgin, and I didn't expect her to be, but I don't exactly want to hear about the guys she's been with. Plus, I'm not too sure I want to hear how even "the perfect guy" wasn't good enough for her parents. If *Paul* wasn't good enough, there's no way in hell they'd accept me.

"So anyway," she continues, oddly dipping her sausage in ketchup, "he was totally clean cut, and my parents quizzed him on his lineage. His *lineage.* As if being valedictorian of his private school and pre-law with early acceptance to pretty much any law school he wanted wasn't enough, he had to have an excellent pedigree as well. The shit really hit the fan when they found out he was from 'new money.' I swear, my parents are certifiable."

"Can't argue with that," I agree.

"Look, I know this is fast. I mean we only just committed to doing this, and I'm already throwing you to the wolves. It's just...this decision could really set me apart from them, and it really means a lot to me to have your support. To be honest, I'm going to be terrified. I'm going to need you, Jay."

I look into her brown eyes and see the fear in them. Not just fear of her parents, but fear of the unknown. Fear of taking a giant, blind leap of faith and not knowing where she's going to land. It suddenly makes me realize that my worries about meeting her parents aren't all that large or important. What's important is sitting right in front of me, and as long as she's by my side—as long as we're by each other's side—I have a feeling everything is going to be okay.

I squeeze her hand. "I've got you, Sunshine. We're a team, right?" Her answering smile is totally worth suppressing my own qualms and being there for her.

"Yeah, we're a team. Me and you against the world!" She shouts the last part, pumping her free fist in the air. She's so serious most of the time, I absolutely love it when she acts like a goofball.

"You're a goober," I tell her, laughing at her antics.

"Yeah, but you love it," she says, returning to her breakfast.

Yeah...I do love it...and I'm pretty sure I love her, too.

Chapter Twenty-Seven

Kate

Jeez, I was on the verge of freaking out this morning when Jay asked if I meant what I said last night. For half a moment, I thought that he may have Googled what I'd said in French and gotten the translation. That would have been mortifying!

Sure, there had been a few, small harmless things like asking him if he knew I spoke French, telling him he's sexy, that it felt good, and begging him not to stop his ministrations. But I may have also let it slip that I was falling in love with him. Maybe...just a little bit.

Thank goodness he'd only been referring to my change in major. I don't think either of us are ready for the L word.

But I can't dwell on that because I got some great news this morning! Casey has finally agreed to go on the transplant list! I completely broke down when her mom and Decker shared the news with me. Was it my tough love? I don't know...and I don't care either. My best friend is choosing to fight! I feel like I could walk on water right about now.

Right now, Jay and I are hanging out at mine and Casey's apartment with Mrs. Evans and Decker while Casey gets some much needed rest. She's still in the hospital, and usually, one of them always holds vigil at Casey's bedside, but she was asleep when Decker offered to drive her mom home, and Mrs. Evans made him come inside to take a shower and begged him to get some decent rest. He'd agreed to the shower, but declined the rest. He would only sleep at the hospital. It's sweet, in a totally stubborn way...he and Casey are *so* perfect for each other. And now they might have a chance.

When they'd arrived and found Jay and me at the apartment doing laundry and collecting more of my clothes to bring back to Jay's, Mrs. Evans ordered a pizza and insisted we all eat together. After the pizza, Jay and Decker remain at the table and play cards while Mrs. Evans and I retreat to the couch.

"How've you been, sweetie?" she asks me, taking my hand.

We're sitting side by side on the couch, facing each other with our legs tucked under our bottoms. It's a position I've sat in with Casey too many times to count, sharing our woes about school, work, boys, and everything else. The memories flip through my mind like a slide show and before I know it, I'm a sobbing mess being cradled in Mrs. Evans' arms.

"I was so mean to her," I cry, drawing the attention of Jay and Decker. I absently note that Jay is off his chair and by my side in seconds, his hand rubbing circles on my back while Mrs. Evans runs hers through my hair.

"Shh," Mrs. Evans soothes. "Kate, sweetheart, you can't beat yourself up over that. You were under duress. It was a long day and a lot had happened. Lord knows my stubborn daughter doesn't make it easy for any of us," I hear Decker laugh and mumble something in the background.

"She's right, Kate," Decker says, sounding closer now.

I sit up and wipe my eyes and face. Jay sits behind me on the couch, and I settle into his embrace, then look up at Decker. "She still didn't deserve me unloading on her like that after a cardiac episode. She had just woken up...she was weak." My eyes well up with tears again.

Decker squats down to my level. "Kate...I think we've all said some things to Casey this week that were a bit harsh. In her defense, she's going through something none of us understand, but at the same time, we all wished she would pull her head out of her ass and see what we see. I know I've gotten more than a little frustrated with her myself."

"Me, too." Mrs. Evans adds. "Kate, you've heard the conversations Casey's father and I have had with her over the years. They weren't always patient and kind. That was the second time you experienced something like this with her, you were scared. I think anger and frustration were natural reactions."

"Now that she's agreed to the transplant, she's probably feeling like a butthead anyway," Decker says, smiling. I'm not sure I've seen him smile so much since he'd arrived on our doorstep. "You should go see her."

"You think she wants to see me?" I ask doubtfully.

"Oh, I know she does. I think she realizes the kind of stress her condition has put you in over the years...the added responsibility. Plus, I think she misses her best friend."

"I thought you were her best friend?" I ask, quirking my eyebrow at him. He's pretty territorial.

"Nah," he says with a wink. "I'm her boyfriend."

My eyes light up and, if possible, his smile widens. "Really?" I squeal, clapping my hands in front of me like a fool.

"Really."

A few more tears slip from my eyes, but this time they're tears of joy. "I'm so happy for you, Decker."

He stands up, looking about ten feet tall. "My work here is done. I'm gonna head back. You," he says, pointing at me, "go see her tomorrow."

I smile and nod. We say goodnight to Decker, and Jay and I decide to spend the night at the apartment with Casey's mom. We watch reruns of *The Golden Girls* and *The Nanny*, much to Jay's chagrin, and eat lots of ice cream.

The only thing missing is Casey...and her boyfriend.

***

After standing outside Casey's hospital room for more than ten minutes, I finally push the door open. I'd passed Decker coming off the elevator, and we chatted for a moment. He said Casey was having a good day. As enthusiastic as I'd been last night about seeing her today, I'm suddenly extremely nervous to come face to face with her.

"Wow, seventeen minutes. That might be a record," I hear Casey say when I step inside. She must think I'm Decker. He said he would grab a bite to eat to give us some time. I pause at the edge of the curtain and peer over at Casey. She's looking at the small, wall-mounted TV; an episode of *Family Feud* is playing.

When I don't respond, she looks over to me, and I smile shyly. We stare at each other for a few moments, then she points the remote at the television and turns it off. The awkward silence continues before we both speak at once.

"Casey—"

"Kate—"

I close my mouth, waiting for her to continue. She seems to be doing the same. Catching each other's eye again, we laugh.

Why is this so awkward?

"I'm sorry, Kate," she finally says. "I put you in a bad position, not only recently, but ever since I was first hospitalized and that wasn't fair to do. I realize now how much pressure I put on you. How much you must have needed to be on alert with me, not knowing what may happen. How scared you probably were every time you walked into the apartment or knocked on my bedroom door. I'm so sorry."

Tears drip down Casey's cheeks, and I walk over to the bed, taking her hand, the one without the wires. "I'm sorry, too, Case. I shouldn't have given you an ultimatum. I kind of just lost it, you know? I was terrified. And I didn't mean to stay away so long; I was embarrassed about the way I acted. Jay, Decker, and your mom finally convinced me that you were probably beating yourself up about it as much as I was, and since you couldn't come to me, I should come to you. So I did."

She smiles and squeezes my hand. "I'm glad you did."

I take a seat on the chair beside her bed and look up at her. She looks so different from a few days ago. Lighter...healthier. Choosing to fight looks good on her. "So you and Decker, huh?"

"So you and Jay, huh?" she throws back, smirking at me.

"He's been so wonderful to me these past few days." I confide, so happy to finally be able to speak openly about my relationship with Jay to my best friend.

"That's great. You deserve something wonderful, Kate."

"You do, too, you know?" I tell her.

"I know," she nods. "And I've got Decker now."

"I don't think you ever didn't have Decker. That boy is crazy about you."

"I'm kinda crazy about him, too." Her cheeks turn rosy from her blush.

"So are you two together now?" I ask, leaving out the fact that Decker had already spilled the beans. I know this is something she'll want to share herself.

“Yeah. We’re together. We’re going to see what happens.”

I can’t help it, I roll my eyes. “Like we all don’t know what’s going to happen. Yours is the forever kind of love, Case. Y’all have loved each other your whole lives, in one way or another. That’s jump-in-front-of-a-bullet kind of love.” She smiles a dreamy smile, and I just know she’s imagining the new idea of a forever with Decker. “Jeez, you’ve got that same goofy look on your face as your boyfriend.” I laugh, and she joins me.

“So tell me more about Jay,” she asks after we sober up.

I smile; this is what I’ve been missing the last few days. Girl talk with my bestie. “Well, I think I told you he’s a mechanic.” Casey nods, remembering our conversation at the apartment a week ago. “He works on motorcycles, and he’s really good at it. Sometimes at night he just rambles on and on about a job he’s working on, and I have no idea what he’s saying but I just love listening to him talk.”

We giggle and laugh and hold nothing back as we share stories of our new relationships. Well…I hold something back. There’s still one thing about Jay I’m not sure how to tell her. I’m not sure what she’ll say or how she’ll react. I hope she’ll be understanding, but it would be a natural response for her to freak out a little bit…to worry.

One day I’ll tell her…just not today.

Chapter Twenty-Eight

Jay

The past couple weeks have been a whirlwind. Casey underwent open heart surgery and received a new heart the day after she and Kate reconciled. She's recovering well and Kate has been visiting her in the hospital nearly every day. I've gotten to know Decker a little bit as we've been spending time together in the cafeteria while the girls have their girl time, doing whatever it is girls do—or whatever they manage to do within the confines of a hospital room. He's a pretty cool guy, and I think I can call him a friend now.

It's kind of weird...making new friends. It just goes to show you that life does go on, despite what has been thrown at you...what you've been through. Now, in addition to Sean, I've got Tom, Johnny, and Decker; a small, but very decent, group of people to choose from when I need a distraction from missing Kate.

And I do miss her...a lot. Since she's adamant about changing majors, she dropped her classes for the new semester. A fact that would send her parents on the attack if they actually were involved in her life. Instead of school, she's taken on more hours at Five, wanting to pad her bank account for when she's inevitably cut off by her parents. She's also been spending a lot of time researching and applying to teaching programs for the fall. I'm so proud of her for finally following her passion.

And passionate she is. We spend every night together now at either her place or mine. Since making her peace with Casey, and Casey's positive health reports, she hasn't been as scared of being in her apartment. It's as though she's finally able to let go of the fear of walking in and finding her roommate unconscious. It *is* a little awkward with Casey's mom sleeping in the next room though. So on the nights where she really needs to let loose, Kate insists we go to my place. I don't argue. Not at all. My girl can get loud, and it turns me on like you wouldn't believe when she can't contain herself.

Tonight, I'm taking her out on a real date. I got a pretty awesome cash tip from a customer, and I can't think of anything—or anyone—that I want to spend it on more. Kate has stood by my side, not just since I've been in California, but for years. She's given me a second chance. She's believed in me. I want to take her out to a nice dinner to show her my appreciation. Plus, she can use a nice night out. She's been working herself to the bone, and with Casey being released next week and her parents' visit shortly after, she's going to be stressed. She needs this. I only wish I could do more.

I arrive at her apartment complex to pick her up at five o'clock on the dot and park my bike in the lot, hurriedly climbing the stairs to her apartment. When we made the date, I'd told her I wanted to take her car. I don't want to drive to San Francisco with her on my bike, especially when she'll be dressed up all nice. I'd made reservations at this little Italian place in San Francisco Decker had raved about. It's about an hour drive, and I'd built in an extra thirty minutes to allow for traffic, parking, and walking.

My mouth drops when she opens the door. She looks beautiful, and it's as if I'm taking a walk down memory lane because she's wearing a white sundress and white sandals, just like she'd had on the day we first met. I can't be sure—because my memory isn't *that* great—but it may even be the exact same ones. Her golden locks gently touch her shoulders and her brown eyes are sparkling.

She smiles at my speechlessness and leans in to kiss me on my cheek. "Hey, handsome," she says, pulling back and grabbing a small purse from the table just inside the door.

"You clean up nice...not sure I've ever seen you in anything other than jeans."

I shrug, looking down at myself. Yeah, I dressed up for this date. I'm wearing khaki pants—which thankfully hadn't caught any road grime on the ride over—and a black button down shirt.

"You look beautiful," I finally say, taking her hand and weaving my fingers with hers.

She blushes, looking down at the ground. I've seen her naked and said many dirty things to her in the throes of passion, yet she still blushes like a schoolgirl when I call her beautiful. That alone is endearing to me.

"Come on, I made reservations. If we're late they may give our table away." I tug her out of the doorway, waiting as she locks up behind her.

"You made reservations?" she asks with surprise in her voice.

"My girl deserves the very best for our first date," I tell her with a wink, and then I smile as her blush deepens. So beautiful.

As we approach her BMW, she tosses me the keys, and I use the fob to unlock the doors. Like a gentleman, I open the passenger door for her and kiss her cheek once she's settled inside. She gives me a shy smile as I close the door, and, out of the corner of my eye, I see her watching me curiously as I walk around the front of the car and let myself in to the driver's side.

Once my seat belt is secured, I look over at her. She's still eyeing me with a puzzled expression on her face. "What?"

"What's up with you tonight?" she asks.

"What do you mean?"

"You're all dressed up, making dinner reservations, opening my door…"

I frown. Am I doing something wrong? Granted, I've never been on a real date before, but I thought this is how the guys did it in the movies.

"Don't get me wrong," she says quickly, placing her hand on my arm. "This is all very nice, very…special."

"So what's the problem?" I ask with some unintentional bite in my tone.

I inwardly curse as Kate winces back. Two minutes into our date, and I'm already fucking it up.

"There's no problem," she says quietly…cautiously. "It's just that I like the real you, Jay. I appreciate all this," she says, gesturing around us, "but I don't want you to feel as though you have to do stuff like this all the time."

I sigh. "I'm sorry, Kate. I just wanted to do something special for you. We've never been on a real date, and I wanted to do something nice."

She shakes her head. “No. I’m sorry. I’m screwing this up. Of course you can do something nice for me. I don’t mean to seem ungrateful. You just seem so...uncomfortable?”

I let out a laugh and run a finger between my collar and my neck. “Yeah...I can’t imagine if I’d ever have to wear a suit.” She laughs, too, and just like that, the tension is broken. I look into her eyes, sobering up. “I’d do it for you, though, Kate. I’m pretty sure I’d do anything for you.”

Kate leans over the console and places her warm hands on my face. “I’m pretty sure I’d do anything for you, too.” Then she presses her lips against mine.

Heaven. This girl is my heaven.

Chapter Twenty-Nine

Kate

The restaurant and dinner are lovely, as is the company. Jay has gone through so much to make tonight perfect for me—for us—that I can't bear to tell him I've been here several times before. Who does he think made the recommendation to Decker and Casey in the first place? No, I won't tell him that. The evening had already gotten off with a rocky start due to me and my big mouth.

I order something I haven't had before, a rich risotto dish, and Jay chooses cannelloni. Judging by the way we're both silent during the meal, I'm guessing his food is as excellent as mine. We share tiramisu for desert with the recommended dessert wine, and I smile as Jay groans when I lick my fork clean.

After dinner, we hold hands walking through the streets of San Francisco. I tell him about my favorite places to visit, restaurants, and dessert shops. We pause along the railing at the edge of the bay and look up at the massive Golden Gate Bridge. It's a sight that never fails to awe me.

"You ever been up there?" Jay asks, tipping his chin to the bridge.

"Dozens of times," I smile, reflecting over walking and biking the bridge my freshman year of college. "It was one of the first places I visited when I arrived in California."

"I don't know why they call it 'The Golden Gate Bridge.' It's orange," he says.

"It's named for the Golden Gate Strait, not the color," I laugh.

He seems to consider this, then looks down at me with a smirk. "Smarty pants." I giggle, then shiver, running my hands up and down my arms. Jay looks at me with concern. "Why didn't you tell me you were cold?"

"I didn't feel it until just now. It's probably the breeze from the bay."

He puts his arm around my shoulder and pulls me into his side, his body warmth immediately pouring out onto me. "Come on, let's head back to the car."

"But I'm having so much fun," I whine.

"We'll have more fun at home, trust me."

This time when I shiver, it has nothing to do with the temperature.

***

After returning my car to the parking lot at my apartment, we go straight to Jay's bike and ride over to his place. I've been staying there so often lately that I've taken over one of the drawers of his small dresser. If it freaks him out, he hasn't said. For someone who had been so uncomfortable with the idea of me even seeing where he lives, he sure seems happy to have me in his space these days. I'd told him he had nothing to worry about.

I pull a pair of pajamas out of *my* drawer and head to the bathroom to change, but Jay stops me in my tracks. He pulls the clothes out of my hands and sets them on the dresser behind me, then he takes a step back and his eyes take me in from head to toe. My skin prickles, as if it can feel his gaze.

He reaches out a hand and runs his fingertip under the strap of my sundress. "You know what I thought about when I first saw you tonight?"

I shake my head in response...not because I don't know, but because I want to hear him say it. I want to hear him tell me that day meant as much to him as it did to me. So much so that he remembers what I'd been wearing. You don't remember those kind of details if the event hadn't been impactful.

"I thought about the first moment I saw you, standing on the side of the road. You were wearing a dress just like this...same color and everything. Same kind of shoes, too. You looked so beautiful, but so frustrated."

I laugh. I was so frustrated. Stupid car. "It *is* the same dress," I tell him and his eyes, filled with heat, widen.

"I thought so, but I couldn't be sure. You kept it?"

"Same shoes, too," I whisper.

He looks down to my feet and a small smile appears on his face. "You got the smudge off?"

My heart flutters. He remembers the smudge on my shoe? I hadn't realized he noticed, but I'm beginning to realize that Jay notices everything.

"They're my favorite sandals," I shrug. "I couldn't part with the dress. That entire day was so crazy...so random. It felt like magic."

"Magic?" he asks, raising a skeptical eyebrow.

"Yeah..." I say, trailing off. How do I explain it to him without sounding like a complete fool? "My whole life, everything has always been so planned. Everything has been so...scientific. Everything made sense and nothing was left to chance. Everything that happened the day you and I met went against the grain. It had to have been magic."

He smiles indulgently at me, placing his hands on my hips. "I guess I can't argue with that." He leans in so his mouth is right beside my ear and whispers, "Want to know what I was thinking when I saw you that day?"

I eagerly nod my head, and he chuckles, his warm breath against my ear and neck causing me to shudder with anticipation.

"I was thinking about how good this dress would look off of you." He punctuates that statement with a nip at my earlobe and my knees buckle. He pulls me tight against his body and I arch my back so I'm completely pressed against him.

"What are you waiting for?" I purr.

Apparently, that cue from me is exactly what he'd been waiting for. Jay drops to his knees in front of me and makes quick work of the straps of my shoes, pulling them off one by one and tossing them over his shoulder. I giggle as one knocks over a small lamp and Jay turns his heated eyes on me as he slowly rises.

"Something funny?"

I stop laughing and shake my head. He smirks as he glides the straps of my sundress off my shoulders, then reaches his arms around my back to lower the zipper. The zipper is pretty well concealed and I smile to myself realizing he must have been paying pretty close attention throughout the night to figure out how to get it off me.

Once the dress pools at my feet, he takes a step back and eyes me in my white, lace strapless bra and matching panties. I hear him hiss in a breath before he says, "You look so fucking innocent."

I step out of the circle of fabric at my feet and close the distance between us. "But you know better than that."

He nods. "I do now."

Truth is, I may still be naïve when it comes to some things, but I *am* a woman who knows what she wants. I may have only had a few partners, but I enjoy sex. It makes me feel good. Until Jay, it had always been about physical release. But now...now it's something else. Something more.

He trails his hand softly down my cheek, and I tilt my face into his palm. "You're something else, Kate," he says, his eyes turning softer now.

"So are you," I tell him, looking deep into his silver eyes.

His brows furrow and, judging by the emotions playing across his face, it seems as though he's thinking something through. A moment later his eyes finally widen with some sort of realization. "Kate...I love you."

Tears fill my eyes. He *loves* me. I hadn't been sure I'd ever hear those words from him. That either of us would ever be ready. Our childhoods were both so devoid of love. Yet we'd found each other, and together, we'd found love.

The logical side of me is wondering if it's too soon, while the other side is shouting, "Who the hell cares? The man loves you!"

"I love you, too," I tell him, pressing a soft kiss to his lips.

"But you're crying," he says with a frown as he pulls away, brushing a tear off my cheek.

"They're happy tears. I promise," I smile, and he returns it with a brand new smile for me. It's the most heart-stopping, genuine smile I've ever seen on his face.

"I love you," he says again, this time it comes out much more easily than the first.

I laugh, "I love you, too."

He picks me up and I wrap my legs around his waist as we spin around, before we collapse onto his bed, both of us laughing like this is the greatest thing that's ever happened.

And it is…it really is.

Chapter Thirty

Jay

"Are you almost ready?"

I turn from the mirror, my hands still messing with the knot around my neck, and look at Kate as she steps into the room. She looks beautiful...different, but beautiful. She's wearing a pastel blue skirt and a white, short sleeve sweater. She's dressing up for this lunch with her parents, as am I.

She quirks her brow, eyeing the mess around my neck. "Need some help, handsome?"

I release a frustrated sigh. "Yes," I tell her, dropping my hands to my sides. Her parents aren't going to like me one way or the other, so I'm not sure what difference it makes that

I'm wearing a tie—a suit—but she asked, and I'd do anything for her.

"Thank you for doing this," she says quietly as she adjusts the noose around my neck.

"I'd do anything for you," I say, echoing my thoughts.

She smiles. "Hopefully, it will be quick and painless. Lots of passive aggressiveness, I'm sure, but they care far too much about appearances to act out in public. The restaurant we're meeting them at is well attended by their friends." She does a final tweak and taps the finished knot. "All set."

I give her a tight smile and pick up the matching suit jacket. Kate had insisted on purchasing the entire get up, saying "You never knew when you might need a suit." I hate that she'd spent the money, but it's difficult to argue with her, especially when she's on her knees and has a very important part of my anatomy between her lips.

"You look so hot," she says, roaming her eyes from the toes of my brand new Italian leather shoes, over the Armani suit, and landing on my face.

"Miss Dumont, if you keep looking at me like you want to eat me, we won't be leaving this apartment," I tell her, closing the distance between us.

"Hmm...don't tempt me. That's a far better offer than seeing my folks." She smooths my lapels and leans in to give me a quick kiss. The three inch heels she's wearing brings her closer to my height and that's about the only part of her stuffy outfit that I love.

Not that she doesn't look gorgeous—she would make a paper bag look good—but this whole wardrobe situation reminds me just how worlds apart we really are. She's Armani and I'm...store brand jeans.

"Come on," she says, tugging on my hand. "I want to get there early to avoid any extra attitude." I groan, but dutifully follow my girl out of her bedroom and down the hall to the living room, where a shrill whistle greets us.

"Lookin' sharp," Casey calls from her place on the couch. She was released from the hospital a few days ago, so Kate and I have been spending more time over here than at my place so Kate can help out. Decker's pretty much got everything covered, but I think Kate just misses her friend.

Kate smiles and tosses Casey her phone. "Take our picture." She scoots up against my side and places her hand on my chest. I put my arm around her waist and tug her closer. I feel like I can never get her close enough. She looks up at me with love in her eyes as I look down at her, my eyes undoubtedly reflecting the same. The click of the phone's camera breaks our stare and we smile at Casey for a few shots.

"You guys are so cute together," Casey coos with...tears in her eyes? What the hell?

“Your new heart has turned you into mush,” Kate teases.

“Baby, she’s being mean to me,” Casey whines to Decker, who is at the other end of the couch rubbing her feet.

Decker rolls his eyes when Casey isn’t looking. “It’s okay, babe. She doesn’t mean it. You have the sweetest heart.” Casey smiles at him and sticks her tongue out at Kate.

Kate laughs and takes my hand again. “Okay, we have to go. Wish us luck.”

“Good luck!” Casey and Decker both call just before the door shuts behind us.

I tense as they say it, knowing that we’ll need all the luck we can get.

***

We arrive at the restaurant twenty minutes early and the maître d’ tells us her parents have already been seated. Kate squeezes my hand a little tighter; her nerves almost as bad as mine. We follow the man through the main dining room to a smaller, more private room in the back. There are a few tables here, and only one is occupied.

By her parents.

They don’t stand to greet their daughter—who they haven’t seen in months—Kate simply rounds the table, kissing them both on the cheek, before returning to my side.

“Father, Mother, this is my boyfriend, Jay Spencer.”

“It’s nice to meet you Dr. and Mrs. Dumont,” I tell them. On the car ride here, Kate had emphasized how important it would be to her father to be addressed as doctor instead of mister. I couldn’t care less what was important to the man since it clearly wasn’t his daughter, but Kate had asked and…you get the idea.

Kate deflates as they barely spare me a glance. Her father checks his watch, as if he’s got some place better to be, while her mother taps her manicured fingernails against the white table cloth. No words have been spoken by either of them. Not even in greeting to their daughter. How Kate turned into a normal, caring, wonderful human being amazes me given that these are the people she grew up with.

We take our seats, and when the waiter approaches to fill our water glasses, Kate’s father orders our meal. Yes, he orders *our* meal. I have no idea what he says, since he’s speaking French, I only hope Kate will warn me if it’s dog shit.

The waiter leaves, and the table is quiet. I’m waiting for Kate to tell her parents about school and wondering if she’ll do it before or after dinner. Hell, I’m not even sure they’d listen if she started speaking.

“I have something I’d like to talk to you both about,” Kate says after a few tense, quiet minutes.

"Does it have anything to do with why you have not enrolled in the summer semester? I spoke with the Dean at the banquet the night before last. He's concerned."

I note how her mother says the dean is concerned but doesn't mention her own concern. Does she have any?

Kate pales, clearly surprised—and maybe embarrassed—her mother spoke to the dean. "Yes, Mother. It does have to do with that. I've been doing a lot of thinking."

"Well, that's your problem right there," her father interrupts. "The only thinking you should be doing is about your schoolwork. The top medical universities in the country are not going to accept a student with less than a 4.0. You also need to quit that...*job*...of yours and put in some hours in a medical facility. Get some experience." He says "job" as though it's shit on the bottom of his shoe.

I look over to Kate and immediately want to grab her hand and drag her out of this place and away from them. Her shoulders are drooped and her head is bowed. She's folding in on herself. I place my hand over hers on her lap and squeeze, lending her my support, she looks up and gives me a small smile. When I raise my eyes back to the table, I catch her mother shooting me a glare, clearly not missing my moment with her daughter.

"I don't want to go to med school anymore," Kate says quietly, but boldly, meeting her father's stare. I'm so proud of her in this moment.

"That's ludicrous. Of course, you're going to med school," he says.

"I want to teach. I want to be a teacher."

"Are you tutoring again? Is that what this is about?" her father seethes. Seriously, how she can share DNA with these two cold as ice people, I'll never know.

"Yes, I'm still tutoring, but that's not what this is about. I'm not passionate about medicine. Not like you are. I'm passionate about teaching. About helping others learn. It's what I want to do."

"No," her father says, his tone final.

Kate's shoulders drop once more, and I can tell she feels defeated. She doesn't need their damn approval. Fuck them.

I push my chair back, not caring about the noise it makes as it scrapes across the marble floor. Kate looks up at me in surprise, and I reach out my hand. "Come on, Sunshine."

"What are you doing?" her father asks, rising from his seat.

"I'm taking Kate home."

"I don't know who the hell you think you are," he says before his wife, who has been otherwise silent, speaks.

"You're the reason for all this, aren't you?" she says, her tone as icy as her demeanor.

"Mother, it's not Jay's fault," Kate tells her, taking my hand and standing up beside me. "This is what I want. It's what will make me happy."

"You can't be serious about this...this boy," her mother says, gesturing to me.

"I am serious about this *man*, Mother. I love him." I squeeze her hand as my chest swells with pride for this girl...my girl.

"Oh, don't be ridiculous, Katherine. He's a felon, for crying out loud."

Suddenly, it feels like the earth has stopped moving.

She knows. Her mother knows.

Chapter Thirty-One

Kate

"He was in the wrong place at the wrong time. It wasn't his fault," I spit out, turning from the table—from my parents—and storming out of the restaurant, dragging Jay behind me.

The nerve! The absolute nerve of her—of both of them and their rotten attitudes! It's one thing to say it to me, I'm used to the verbal abuse...but to take it out on Jay, to blame him? It appalls me. How she knows about his past, I have no idea. She probably has someone spying on me, and it wouldn't be too difficult for her to get information on him since she's an attorney and has friends in high places. Bullshit. It's such bullshit.

"I'm so sorry," I tell Jay once we get to my car. "Gah! They're assholes. They're such assholes. And my mother was so out of line...calling you a felon."

"It's not a lie, Kate."

I sigh as I lean back against my car door. I look at Jay; he looks so defeated. "I know, but it was a shitty thing for her to do. To blame you and then call you that like it's the only thing that defines you."

"Let's just go home," he says, opening the passenger door to let me in. He then gets in the driver's side and starts the drive back to my apartment. It's a short ride, but in that brief time I note that he's acting different. He's quiet.

Why do I have the feeling that everything is about to change?

***

When we get to my apartment, Jay quietly follows me up the stairs. At least he's coming in. He didn't go straight for his bike and head home. That's a good sign...right?

Casey and Decker are still on the couch when we walk in and both look over from the television with surprise in their eyes.

"Back so soon?" Casey asks.

I just shake my head, indicating that now is not a good time, and lead Jay to my bedroom.

“I’m gonna change,” he says, grabbing his jeans and t-shirt off my bed and heading to the bathroom. It’s the first thing he’s said since we left the restaurant, and I feel like it might be one of the last things he will say to me, too. And I know it seems silly, but why wouldn’t he just change in here? We’ve already seen each other naked multiple times.

What the hell just happened? Yes, my parents were assholes, but we’d prepared for that—planned for it. We knew that part would be inevitable. Sure, we hadn’t anticipated that my mother would have done some digging into Jay’s history, but it’s not like it was a secret between him and me.

I take a seat on the edge of my bed and wait for him to return...because he will return. He won’t just leave. Will he? I relax as I hear his booted footsteps approaching from the hall.

“Is everything okay?” I ask as he steps into the room.

His suit is folded over his arm, and I stand up to help him put all the pieces back on their hangers. He slips everything inside the garment bag, zips it up, and finally turns to me, looking at the floor.

“I don’t think this is going to work out,” he finally says, causing all the air to rush out of my lungs.

“What? No.” I barely get the words out. It feels as though the earth has stopped moving, and I’m losing my balance. I step back and sit on the edge of my bed again, my legs no longer able to hold me up.

“We’re so different...you and I...we’re from two different worlds, Kate.”

“Is this about my parents?” Of course, it’s about my parents. “What they think doesn’t matter to me anymore. You know that.”

“It’s not about them. It’s not *only* about them. Shit. I don’t know.” He scratches the back of his neck and looks anywhere but at me. And that hurts. That hurts a lot.

“I don’t understand.”

“What your mom said,” he continues, “that’s going to happen a lot, Kate. When people find out about me...about what I did...they’re going to look at me differently. And if you’re with me, they’re going to look at you differently, too.”

“You think I care about all that?” I ask, raising my voice. “I don’t. You know I don’t. I’ve never looked at you any different, Jay.”

“I know,” he says sadly. “I know you haven’t, and I know you don’t. But others will and you shouldn’t have that following you around the way that I do.”

“That doesn’t matter to me, Jay. You...you are what matters to me. You’re all that matters to me.”

“That’s not true.”

"It is true," I whisper, tears coming to my eyes. "I'm not ashamed of you, Jay. I love you. I'm not ashamed of you."

"I just can't do this to you, Kate."

"You're not doing anything to me!" I yell, getting to my feet. Why doesn't he understand? His past is just that...it's in the past. What happened to him...it wasn't even his fault.

He just shakes his head. "There are things I'll never be able to do Kate...places I'll never be able to go...all because I have to check a little box that says I've been convicted of a felony. I've already come to grips of what that means for me; I won't let it limit you as well."

"But Jay, it won't limit me. It won't," I plead.

"Yeah? What happens when you get the teaching job you love and one of your coworkers finds out that your boyfriend is a felon? Or if it turns up on a background check that you're associated with me. What happens then? What happens if you lose your job?"

I shake my head, tears spilling down my cheeks now. "That won't happen."

"It can."

"It won't!"

"Kate, I've been living in a bubble here with you. What we have...had...it was amazing."

His use of past tense nearly kills me. “It *is* amazing. Why are you doing this?”

“I’m doing this for you, Sunshine.”

“Don’t call me that! You don’t get to call me that if you’re breaking up with me!” I cry.

I fall to my knees and sob. I don’t understand. Things were so perfect this morning. Sure we were full of nerves, but we were full of love, too.

“I love you,” I say through my sobs. “Please don’t leave me.”

Chapter Thirty-Two

Jay

Her tears nearly undo me. I don't want to hurt her. God...I love her...I just don't want to make her life more complicated. I'd meant what I said, I don't want her to have to one day choose between me and her passion because of a stupid decision I'd made when I was eighteen years old.

"I'm sorry, Kate. I'm so sorry."

"Please," she begs, looking up at me from the floor. Her cheeks are streaked with mascara from her tears. "Please don't do this. I don't want to be without you."

"You'll be better off without me," I say, kneeling down in front of her. I can't look down at her like that. I just can't. "Kate, you're going to do amazing things. You're going to be an amazing teacher. You're going to be that teacher that makes a difference in kids' lives. The one they remember twenty years later because she listened to them and cared about them. In the long run, I'd only weigh you down."

"You won't."

"I will."

"You won't! Dammit, I won't let you!"

She throws herself at my chest and wraps her arms around me. Her body shaking with her sobs. I want to wrap my arms around her. I want to comfort her. I want to forget all about this and just be selfish. But I can't. This is what's best for Kate. It's not even about me, not really. It's about her.

"Kate, this shit is going to follow me around like a black cloud for the rest of my life. It's never going to be off my record. Ever. That's something *I* have to live with, not you."

"This isn't new information, Jay. Why now? Why are you doing this now? What has changed? What happened today that made you feel like you're not good enough for me all of a sudden? I thought we were past this."

I want to laugh. All of a sudden? Past this? "Kate, I've never felt like I was good enough for you."

She pulls away from me and looks into my eyes, a frown on her beautiful, tear-soaked face. "You've never felt like you were good enough for me? Did I make you feel that way?"

I shake my head. "Never."

"Then why? Why would you feel that way?"

She really doesn't get it. I abruptly stand up and place my hands on the back of my head. I hate this. I hate this situation. I hate that I let myself get so close...that I let *her* get so close...that I let myself fall in love...that I let *her* fall in love. Fuck!

"I'm a convicted felon, Kate!" I yell. "What part of that don't you understand? It's not all rainbows and fucking butterflies in my life. People judge me. People move to the other side of the street when they see people like me coming. There are places I can't get jobs. I can't pass simple background checks. I can't vote. There's a stigma that's always going to be attached to me. Forever. If you're with me, that's going to be attached to you, too. Don't you get that?"

More tears fall from her eyes, and I continue to feel like an asshole. But seriously...can't she see? I'm doing this for her!

"I want you in my life, Jay. I don't care what other people think. I don't care if other people can't accept it. I don't care if I have to change jobs because some stuck-up assholes believe that one mistake defines a person. Those aren't people I want to associate with."

Her words make me love her more, if that's even possible, but they also frustrate the hell out of me. She's not making this easy.

But why should it be easy? Why should breaking someone's heart be easy? Especially the one person—other than my best friend and brother—who has always been there for me. It should be difficult. It should fucking hurt.

Kate gets to her feet and steps up to me. I take a step back.

"Jay, please."

"No. This is how it has to be."

"But I love you, and you love me. You can't leave now; we've only just found each other!"

"I don't love you, Kate," I lie. "I thought I did, but I don't. Hell, I don't even think I know what love is."

"That's not true. You're lying! Why are you lying?" She keeps stepping towards me, and I keep stepping back. "Stop moving away from me. Please don't do this."

There's only one way I know she'll let me leave. It's a shitty thing to do, and it makes me sick, but I'd rather her be mad at me and hate me than be heartbroken.

"I never loved you, Kate. I just said what I needed to in order to get what I wanted from you."

She stops moving. “What? What are you saying? What do you mean?”

“Three years in prison...it’s a long time to be without a woman. I had been thinking about you for a while. I did what I had to do.” It’s a complete and total lie. Yes, I dreamed about the girl with the long blonde hair and beautiful brown eyes, but I never thought to use her in the way I was implying.

She shakes her head. “No. I don’t believe that. You’re lying.”

“It’s the truth. Believe what you want,” I shrug, displaying my indifference. The slap that follows is both painful and freeing. Painful because it was right across my face, freeing because now I know she’s pissed. Now I know she’ll let me go.

“Get out,” she says quietly. Now, I almost don’t want to leave, knowing that this is truly the end, but that’s just me being selfish again. “Get out!”

I take one long last look at her, knowing I’m never going to see her again, and walk out the door.

I pass a wide-eyed Casey and Decker, who I’d forgotten were even in the apartment, and go to pick up my helmet. Out of the corner of my eye, I see Casey take off down the hall, probably for Kate’s room, but Decker is still standing there...watching me.

“That was all bullshit, wasn’t it?” he says. I ignore him as I pull on my leather jacket.

"Casey pulled the same shit with me. Tried to push me away for my own good because she was sick and didn't want me to be miserable. She didn't give me any credit that I could handle it. You're doing the same thing. You're not giving Kate any credit. She's tougher than she looks."

Don't I know it...

"Take care of them," I tell Decker as I walk out the door for the last time.

***

I should probably be concerned that I don't remember the ride back to my hole-in-the-wall apartment. But the truth is, I don't really give a shit about anything right now.

Once inside my apartment I start packing my bag, grateful I'd picked up that pull-behind for mine and Sean's trip to Sturgis since I've accumulated more shit since moving here. I'll leave most of the household stuff, but I'm taking everything else. Except Kate's drawer. I'll bag that up and drop it outside her apartment before I go. She left her little pink duffel bag here a while back.

I get everything set up on my bike and leave my apartment key in an envelope with next month's rent and a note, and slide it under the super's door. He'll probably pocket the cash, but I don't really care. I'm getting the hell out of here.

I make sure the rigging for the pull-behind is secure and hop on my bike. I ride over to

Kate's place and park around the corner, I don't want her to hear my bike. If she comes out…if I see her again, even for a second, even from afar, I'm not sure I'll be able to keep up the charade. I sneak up the stairs and leave her bag outside the apartment door, pausing for a moment.

"Goodbye, Kate," I whisper to the closed door.

I head back to my bike and get on the highway heading east…it's time to go home.

Chapter Thirty-Three

Kate

I'm still lying in a heap on my floor when Casey comes in.

"Kate?" Her voice is full of concern, and it makes me cry harder. "I'm so sorry, sweetie. We didn't mean to eavesdrop, but it was hard not to overhear." She's on the floor beside me now, rubbing my back. It's a gesture a mother would make to comfort her child, I guess, if I had any idea what a caring mother was like.

"Do you want to talk about it?"

"He left me," I sob.

"I know, hun. I'm sorry."

"I love him."

"I know you do. I think he loves you, too. I think he's just scared. I don't think he meant the things he said."

"Then why say them?"

"Because he was afraid. Afraid of being with you...afraid of hurting you...afraid of losing you. That's how it was for me when things got real intense with Decker. I was scared to death that my secrets would hurt Decker, so I pushed him away."

I remember just a few weeks ago when Casey and Decker had gotten into their fight right before Casey ended up in the hospital. She'd pushed him away because he was getting too close to finding out the truth, and she'd freaked out.

"But Jay isn't hiding anything, Case. I already know all his secrets."

She's silent for a moment, then asks, "Was he really in prison?"

I sit up, wanting to look her in the eyes and see her reaction to what I say. I haven't told anyone about Jay's past, it's not relevant to his future—or to mine—but Casey is my best friend. If I'm going to tell anyone, it'll be her.

"Yes," I say, waiting for a reaction. When I don't get one, I relax. See? It's not the end of the world. Why couldn't Jay just see that? Not everyone is going to judge him poorly. At least not those who matter.

“What happened?”

I adjust my position so my back is resting against my bed, and my knees are pulled up to my chest. Casey mimics my position beside me. Taking a deep breath, I tell Casey the truth.

“Jay didn’t always hang out with the best people. One night, shortly after we’d first met, he stopped at a gas station on his way home. It was in a not-so-great part of town, but it was close to the apartment he shared with his brother. He came out of the store after paying, and bumped into an old friend of his. The friend asked Jay for a ride, so Jay gave him one. The guy had a black duffel bag with him and was acting all paranoid; Jay just figured he was on something.”

“Like drugs?” Casey asks with wide eyes. If only that was the worst of it...

I nod my head. “Yeah. Jay didn’t do drugs, but he used to hang out with some guys who did, and he was a bit of a troublemaker. His brother—Mac—is a cop, and he’d been trying to straighten Jay out. It was working, and he was steering clear of that crowd, but he’s a nice guy, and he didn’t think there would be any harm in driving a friend home. Anyway, they had just left the convenience store parking lot when he got pulled over. His friend started freaking out, trying to stuff the bag under the seat.”

Casey’s eyes widen again. “What was in the bag?”

"Money and guns."

"What?!" her mouth drops.

"Turns out his friend had robbed a pawn shop a couple hours earlier. A video camera caught an image of his friend at the pawn shop, and the cop had spotted the guy getting into Jay's car at the gas station. Jay's brother was one of the cops that showed up on the scene."

"But how did Jay end up in jail? He didn't do anything wrong."

"He told them he had no idea, but was his word against theirs. With his history of being a troublemaker, they didn't believe him. And his friend didn't say anything to the contrary. In fact, he said Jay had been waiting to give him a ride after the robbery."

"What a dick!" Casey shrieks.

"Yeah," I nod.

"His brother didn't believe him?"

"He wanted to...but Jay had let him down so much before. Their parents were bad news and weren't around much, so Jay was a wild child. Anyway, the whole thing really put a strain on their relationship for a while. It took Jay a long time to get past the anger of his brother arresting him and not believing him, but eventually he got over it."

"His brother is the one who arrested him?"

"Yeah. His friend was arrested for armed robbery, and Jay was arrested as an accessory."

"Wow, that's pretty rough."

"He was in the wrong place at the wrong time. If he just hadn't stopped for gas or not given his friend that ride, things could have turned out so different."

"If his friend hadn't robbed someone..."

"Yeah, there's that," I agree with a frown. "So, Jay spent over three years in prison for a crime he didn't commit or didn't mean to commit, I guess. We wrote each other letters for a little while. I looked him up at the Department of Corrections website after I'd found out he went to prison," I admit bashfully, feeling like a total stalker. Though he did come to California for me, so I guess we're sort of even now.

"Wait a minute," Casey's eyes dart to mine, suddenly realizing something. "You told me you met him at the restaurant."

I look down at my hands in my lap, feeling incredibly guilty for lying to my friend. I should have known she wouldn't judge Jay, especially once she knew the whole story. I should have just told her the truth back then.

This is exactly one of the things Jay had been afraid of...that I would have to hide our history because I was ashamed of him. But that's not the case at all. I'm not ashamed of him. I just don't want to deal with the attitudes of people who would judge him without knowing him...without knowing the truth. People love jumping to conclusions. That's what I've been afraid of. I've never been ashamed of him. I never would be.

More tears drip down my cheeks, and Casey pulls me into a hug. I take my friend's consolation, careful of the stitches on her chest.

"I'm sorry I lied to you. I was just afraid of what you might think if you knew he'd been in jail, and I didn't want to get mad at you for making a snap judgement."

"I understand," she says. "If I were in your shoes, I'd probably be apprehensive about telling people as well."

"But you're my best friend, I should have trusted that you would hear me out."

Casey shrugs. "It's not a big deal. You would have told me eventually. You *did* tell me eventually. That's what's important."

"I guess so."

"So tell me...how did you meet?"

I smile at the memory. "It was kismet, I swear." Casey squeezes my hand and gives me an encouraging smile. "You know I did a lot of volunteer work in high school. I'd gone to Greenville for the day to help at an event for a free health clinic. Turns out the event was canceled, but no one told me. So I turned around and drove home. I was on I-26 when my car broke down. I had been out there, baking in the sun on the side of the road, when he showed up like a mirage."

I tell Casey all about the short time I'd spent with Jay four years earlier. How he'd helped me on the side of the road, and how we'd met again by chance in the coffee shop and spent hours talking about everything and nothing. Then how he'd stood me up for our dinner date…because he'd been arrested.

That night, when I'd seen his picture on TV, it was because he'd been arrested for armed robbery. The local news had all sorts of foul things to say about him and his "friend." But I swore that wasn't the Jay I'd met. I hadn't spent more than a few hours with him, but I just knew.

Chapter Thirty-Four

Kate

"Wow," Casey says. I'm watching her face, trying to guess what she's thinking. But I can't tell by her expression. She's like a fortress.

"Well?"

"Well what?" she asks.

"Do you think I'm crazy?"

"No, I don't think you're crazy. Fate brought the two of you together…not once, not twice, but *three* times," she said, holding up three fingers for emphasis. "And you believed in him, there's nothing wrong with that."

"That's what I've been trying to tell him."

"I think it's pretty cool, Kate. Unconventional, but cool. I mean who meets the love of their life on the side of the road like that? And he saved you! Total damsel in distress situation and he rocked the white knight role."

I love that she overlooks the fact that he'd been in prison and jumps right for the girly, fairy tale part of the story. But I don't like that she called him the love of my life. That only reminds me that he's gone.

"I have to go to him. I can't let him do this. I have to fight for him."

Casey smiles. "What are you waiting for?"

***

As I step out of the apartment, I freeze. My bag. The one I'd kept at Jay's...it's sitting outside my door.

No.

He is *not* doing this to us. I won't let him.

I race to Jay's apartment in San Jose. I don't see his bike parked near his building, but I don't let that deter me. I race inside and up the stairs and bang on his door for a good five minutes. Surely if he were in there he would have opened the door just to shut me up by now.

Leroy's! I bet he went to the shop to work and blow off some steam or something. Guys like to tinker with engines and stuff when they're upset, right?

I use the map on my phone to locate the garage and drive the couple of blocks over to Leroy's. There are several bikes in the parking lot, which makes sense since it's a bike shop. I can't tell if any of the bikes are his, though. I go into the reception area and an older gentleman, Leroy given the name on his shirt, looks up at me with a sneer.

"Can I help you?" he barks.

"I'm looking for Jay Spencer. Is he here?"

"No, he's not fucking here." Well, isn't Leroy a peach. Jay hadn't mentioned his boss was an asshole.

"Can you tell me when you're expecting him in next?" I ask, desperate to have some sort of lifeline to Jay in case I can't find him myself.

"Try never. He quit."

My jaw drops. "He quit? He loves his job."

Leroy laughs mockingly. "Yeah? Well, not enough."

"When...when did he quit?"

"He called about thirty minutes ago."

I close my eyes. No. No no no no. I can feel the tears welling up behind my eyes, and I need to get out of here. I need to leave.

I turn and race out the door, crashing into a firm chest. "I'm so sorry," I say, walking around the person I crashed into.

"Kate?" I spin around. It's Jay's friend, Johnny.

"Hi, Johnny," I say, trying to keep it together. "You haven't talked to Jay, have you?"

He frowns. "Sorry, Kate. He left. Said he was going back home and...that he's not coming back."

Home. He's going home. He's really through with me. With us. It's over.

"I'm sorry, Kate."

I wipe the fallen tears from my cheeks. "Thanks, Johnny. Take care, okay?"

He gives me a sad smile. "You too, Kate."

I walk to my car in a trance.

He left.

He's gone.

He's not coming back.

He went *home.*

He was *my home.*

I get in my car and lock the doors, then send Casey a text letting her know where I am and letting her know that Jay is gone.

I consider sending Jay a text, but what would be the point? He left. He's gone. He's not coming back. I rest my head on my steering wheel and cry.

I cry for what I lost.

I cry for what we could have had.

I cry for Jay.

And I cry for myself, because I'm not sure I'm ever going to love someone as much as I love him.

I barely register the knocking on my window, but when I look up, I see my best friend's face. How long have I been sitting here? I unlock the door and fall into her arms.

"It's okay," she says, holding me tight. She steers me towards the back door, and we get in the backseat. It's then I notice Decker is here, too. He gets in the driver's seat and takes us home. I cry with my head on my best friend's lap the entire way home.

He left.

He's gone.

He's not coming back.

***

After calling out sick for three days in a row, I quit my job at the restaurant. I have a good pot of cash saved up, and I just don't feel like working anymore. I don't feel like doing anything anymore. I do nothing but sit around the apartment all day eating ice cream, ordering the occasional pizza, and watching horror movies.

Casey's worried about me. I know this. She tried getting me to watch a chick flick the other day, and I yelled at her. Chick flicks are always love stories.

Fuck love.

She's still mostly homebound as she's still recovering, so our shared presence in the apartment is making things a bit crowded. I spend a lot of time in my room.

Alone.

The way it should be.

Chapter Thirty-Five

Jay

One month later…

"How long is it gonna take you to finish that clutch?" Sean asks from the other side of the bay.

"When did you become such a nag?" I retort.

"When you started taking three hours to do an hour job."

I drop my tools to the ground and wipe the sweat off my brow. He's right, I should have been finished with this two hours ago. But I can't fucking concentrate because a certain brown-eyed girl is dancing around in my mind.

Kate.

I can't get her out of my head. The moment I'd arrived back in South Carolina and unpacked my stuff in my old bedroom at Mac's place, I realized what a mistake I'd made.

I miss her. I miss her so fucking bad.

I'm such an idiot. I was such an asshole to her, all because I thought I'd known what was best for her. She's been living with herself her whole life, surely her opinion on what was best for her should have factored in somewhere. I'm such a stubborn, foolish asshole.

"Wanna talk about it?" he asks, walking over to my station.

"Not really."

"Why don't you just call her? Tell her you're sorry and beg for forgiveness."

"What part of 'I don't want to talk about it' didn't you understand, asshole?" I pick up my tools again and start working. I've only got about ten more minutes of work to do, if I actually work and quit daydreaming about Kate and all my mistakes.

In my periphery, I see Sean shaking his head. "Look, you need to get out of your head, man. It's one thing when you channel that shit into your work, but it's another when it gets in the way of your work."

I take a deep breath in and then let it out. "You gonna fire me?"

"Fuck, no," he says, and I breathe a little easier. Right now, this job in Sean's repair shop is the only thing keeping me together. The only thing keeping me from riding my sorry ass back to California to do exactly what he said...beg Kate for forgiveness. Either that or ride my bike right off a bridge—that's my other option.

"I just wish you'd talk to me, bro. You haven't said much of anything since you've been back."

"Not much to say."

"Bullshit."

I tighten the final bolt and start cleaning up my area, ignoring Sean.

"Aren't you going to see if that works?"

"I replaced a clutch, Sean. It's not like it was an engine rebuild."

"You'd think it was the way you were drag-assing it."

I slam the drawer of my tool chest and spin around to face him. "What the fuck is your problem?" I want to slap the smug grin right off his face.

"Now that's more like it," he says, nodding his head. "Show some emotion. Let me know you're still alive in there."

"I'm fuckin' alive, all right?"

He watches me for a minute, then says, "Sweep the floors, asshole. Then we're going to Harry's. No arguments."

I roll my eyes as I nod, knowing there's no way out of it. I toss my grease stained rag onto the counter top and grab the broom, making quick work of the shop floors while Sean closes up the office. He'd opened this place about three years ago, while I was in prison. It was always his hope that we'd work here together. Now we are, although I think we'd both hoped the circumstances would be different.

***

"Talk," Sean demands once we're seated in a booth. Harry's is a rundown bar and grill that has seen better days, but the food is amazing.

I slide my glass of sweet tea between my hands. "Where do I start?"

"How about the part where you fucked up? Last time we talked about your girl, you thought you were in love with her. Next thing I know, you're back here, more sour than a lemon. What happened?"

I give Sean the abbreviated version of what went down between Kate and me. I tell him about the ill-fated lunch with her parents and my subsequent thought process. I tell him what I'd said to her back at her apartment. He can sense my shame from across the table; I can see it in the pity in his eyes.

"From everything you've told me about this girl, she seems like a tough chick. You didn't give her enough credit."

My hands tighten around my glass. "I don't want that life for her. I don't want her to have to worry about what people think about *me* all the damn time."

"Why don't you let her choose what life she wants?"

I shake my head. "She's all caught up in the romance and the love. She's not considering the reality of it all."

"And you are? Sounds to me like you're a little caught up in the romance and the love, too."

I raise an eyebrow at him. "What the fuck are you talking about?"

"The guy version of romance, dude." I stare at him blankly. "We think we know what's best and want to save the women we love from us because we never feel we're good enough for them. It's all self-sacrificing shit like that. What we don't realize is that they don't want to be saved from us, they're the ones that want to save *us* from *ourselves*."

"I'm not sure I'm following."

Sean rolls his eyes as he shakes his head. "The lesson here is this: don't make decisions for your woman. Let her make her own decisions."

"That's deep," I snort, taking a sip of my tea.

"It's the truth. It's why I'm happily married to the love of my life with a baby on the way."

I choke on my drink. "What?"

Sean's smile is a mile wide. "Just found out. Julia's seven weeks pregnant."

"Holy shit, congratulations, man." I lean across the table and pat him on the back.

"Thanks. It's kind of surreal, ya know?"

"I can imagine. You'll be a great dad, bro."

We spend the rest of the time shooting the shit and catching up on things like we would have pre-Kate, when I was just a regular moody bastard, instead of a moody, brokenhearted bastard. He tells me some of the ridiculous baby names Julia has mentioned, and some equally ridiculous ones he's considered.

We also talk a little more about Kate, and by the time we leave Harry's, I feel like I've got a pretty decent plan for getting her back. If only she'll have me...

***

"I'll see you in the A.M.," Sean calls out before setting his helmet on his head and securing the strap. I nod, then do the same. We start our bikes together and pull out into the street. We live in the same part of town, so we'll ride side-by-side most of the way.

I've missed this...riding with Sean, even if it's just the five miles home. It's a camaraderie we share beyond the limits of friendship. A brotherhood, if you will. The only thing that feels better than cruising with my best friend is having my girl on the back of my bike. *My girl.* Hopefully she'll have me back. I run through all the possible scenarios in my mind as I ride. The good, the bad, the—

What the fuck?

We're riding through an intersection and the bright white lights in my peripheral vision, just beyond Sean, are too fucking bright. They're too close. They're blowing through the red light.

Sean!

It all happens so fast, but it seems like slow motion.

I turn my head to the right and meet Sean's wide, terrified eyes. Just beyond him I see the truck. It's close...too close...and getting closer. A horn is blaring somewhere...it sounds like it's miles away.

I meet Sean's eyes again, noting the fear in them, before releasing my throttle. Then it all goes black.

Chapter Thirty-Six

Kate

"Good morning, Sunshine!" Casey calls from my bedroom door.

"Don't call me that!"

She apologizes, looking a little sheepish. "Sorry, hun. I forgot. Up and at 'em, though. I made breakfast."

Once she disappears from the doorway, I roll back over and pull the covers over my head. I am so not in the mood for her happy horseshit attitude today. Casey allowed me exactly five days to wallow in self-pity after Jay left before launching straight into Operation Happy Kate. I tolerate it since I don't really want to get mad at her—at least not to her face—while she's still recovering. But I just can't do it today.

Today I feel...I don't know. Wrong? Off? Maybe it's PMS. Whatever it is, it just doesn't feel right.

"Kate! Get your ass out of bed!" Casey calls from the kitchen.

"Decker! Control your woman!" I call back.

Knowing it's pointless to try to fight with her—she'll win—I roll out from under the covers and stomp my way to the bathroom.

"We have neighbors below us, Kate," Casey sings from the kitchen.

"Fuck 'em," I grumble. I take care of business and brush my teeth before joining Casey and Decker in the kitchen. I glare at Decker, and he just shrugs his shoulders. "Traitor. We're supposed to have solidarity, Deck."

"Sorry," he says, not sounding sorry at all as he scarfs down his omelet.

"Whatever." I plop down in my seat and look at the creation on my plate. Casey has been spending her time researching healthy and heart happy recipes. Most of them are delicious, so I don't complain, but I really miss egg yolks. If I have to eat another egg white omelet, I might scream. "What's in this one?"

"I figured I'd go easy on you today. It's spinach and feta."

I can live with that. I inhale my omelet in less than two minutes and down my juice. "Thanks, Case."

"No problem. So what's on the agenda for today?"

I lean back in my seat and rub my full belly. "I don't know, drill sergeant. What's on the agenda for today?"

"Oh, I don't know. How about burpees?"

"Not a fucking chance."

"You've got some potty mouth on you all of a sudden."

Decker's eyes are darting back and forth between us like he's watching a tennis match. It's actually quite comical.

"It's what happens when your soul is ripped out of your body and stomped on by the one person you thought loved and understood you," I say flatly.

"Hey, now. I love and understand you."

"It's not the same and you know it."

"I think we should go for a walk. It's a beautiful day."

My cell phone starts ringing in my bedroom. Saved by the bell! I briefly wonder who would be calling at seven in the morning, but then I realize I don't care as it gets me out of planning my happy day. "I better go get that," I say, jumping up from the table before

Casey can finalize our daily itinerary. Her Operation Make Kate Happy is more like Operation Keep Kate Busy. Not cool, not cool at all.

I pick up my phone from my nightstand and see that the caller has a South Carolina area code. I contemplate answering. It could be one of my parents. Even though I have their numbers stored, they could be calling me from another line. They've probably realized by now that I blocked their numbers after our little lunch.

The phone stops ringing, making my decision for me. I wait for the caller to leave a message, but the phone starts ringing again. Same number. My parents wouldn't be so persistent. They don't have that kind of time to waste on me.

Could it be Jay? But I have his number stored, too...

The call goes to voicemail, and immediately starts ringing again.

"You gonna get that?"

I turn and see Casey in the doorway. "I don't know who it is. It's a Columbia number."

"Just answer it. They obviously want to speak to you; it hasn't stopped ringing."

I slide my finger across the screen to answer the call. "Hello?"

"Is this Kate?" a frantic, male voice asks.

"Who's this?"

"Ah, you don't know me. My name is Mac Spencer."

"You're Jay's brother," I say quietly, my gut filling with dread. Why is Jay's brother calling me? "Is he okay?"

"There was an accident," he says.

"Where is he?" I ask, my eyes filling with tears.

"Memorial Hospital," he says.

"I'll be there. I'm in California...but I'll be there. I'm leaving now."

"Thank you, Kate. He's just...I think he needs you."

I end the call without saying anything else, and I jump when Casey's hand touches my shoulder.

"What's going on?" she asks, her voice laced with concern.

"I don't know. That was Jay's brother, Mac. He said there was an accident, and Jay's in the hospital."

"Oh my gosh," Casey says, bringing her hands up to her mouth. "Is he okay?"

"I don't know. I have to...go. He needs me. I have to go!"

"Okay. Get dressed, I'll pack you a bag."

I quickly dress in jeans and a t-shirt, then pull my hair back in a scrunchie—hey, don't knock 'em, they don't break my hair like elastics. I don't even look in the mirror; I just grab my bag from Casey, slip on my flip-flops at the door, and run out.

My heart races the entire way to the airport, and it doesn't stop until I'm seated on a plane, in an uncomfortable seat that cost me over $1000. If I'm being honest, as the plane taxis the runway, my heart still hasn't stopped racing. I feel like it's going to beat right out of my chest and the only thing—*the only thing*—that is going to make it stop is laying my eyes on Jay and knowing that he's going to be okay.

Please, please let him be okay.

I'm not a religious person, but I pray the entire cross-country flight.

***

"Kate?" Mac calls out as I enter the hospital. I recognize his voice from the call, and as I turn to look at him, I realize I would have recognized him by sight as well. He's the spitting image of Jay...or Jay is the spitting image of him. They could be mistaken for twins, with the exception of a few extra creases around Mac's eyes.

I go to him. "Where is he?"

"Come with me," he says, taking my hand and pulling me through the crowd of people in the waiting room and down a hall to the elevators.

"Is he okay? Is he hurt? What happened?"

"Physically, he's going to be all right," Mac says once we're in the elevator and ascending to the fourth floor. "Mentally…I don't know. But he's alive. He's okay."

I let out a breath I hadn't realized I'd been holding. I drop my bag by my feet and cover my face with my hands as tears of relief come pouring out.

"I'm sorry, I didn't mean to alarm you. I tried to tell you he's going to be okay, but you'd already hung up the phone."

"What happened? I mean, he's in the hospital, so he got hurt, right?"

Mac nods. "He has a broken arm and a concussion. They've been keeping him for observation, but he should be released tomorrow."

"That's good, right?"

"Yeah, that's real good. He's been responding pretty well to the tests."

"That's good," I agree. But why did Mac call me so urgently and tell me that Jay needs me when all he's got is a broken arm and a concussion? Granted, those can still be very serious injuries, but they're also fairly common. "I don't mean to downplay Jay's injuries and all that, but I'm not sure why you called me here. We didn't exactly part on good terms...I'm not sure he's going to want to see me."

Mac looks away for a moment and swipes his hand under his eye. That sense of dread in my belly is back. What is he not telling me?

"It's Sean."

"Jay's best friend, Sean?"

Mac nods. "My best friend, too."

I hadn't known they were all close. Jay had never mentioned it. "Is he okay?" I ask cautiously.

Mac shakes his head. "He didn't make it."

I cover my gaping mouth with my hand. Oh no. *No.* I can't imagine what Jay must be going through. They'd been in the accident together, and Jay survived, but Sean didn't? He must be beating himself up pretty badly.

"I'm so sorry," I tell him, not knowing what else to say. What can you say?

"Jay's distraught. With good reason. But he won't speak to anyone. He's just...shutting down. Sean told me about you...said you were why Jay went to California after he got off parole. He told me Jay was crazy about you. I just figured...I thought if anyone could get through to him, maybe it would be you."

I take Mac's hand and squeeze it. "I'll do whatever I can," I promise him.

The elevator dings its arrival on the fourth floor, and we get out. Mac leads me down the hall to room 407, and I silently follow him inside. I breathe a sigh of relief seeing Jay in one piece. His arm is in a cast, and he's got a bandage on his forehead, but aside from that he looks okay. He looks like a giant in the tiny hospital bed, though, and I'm sure he's desperate to get out of it and the pale blue gown he's in.

He rolls his head to look over as we enter and his damp eyes widen as they lock on mine. "Kate?"

I step around Mac and tentatively walk towards his bed. He watches me, taking in every messy piece of me as I approach. His eyes are glassy, and when I stop at his bedside, he blinks and a tear spills down his cheek.

I wipe the tear away with my thumb. "Hey, stranger."

He looks at me as though he can't believe I'm actually here. Then he wraps his good arm around my waist and pulls me towards him. I carefully wrap my arms around his neck, holding his head against my chest. "I'm so sorry," he mumbles.

What happens next absolutely breaks my heart. My big, strong, tough guy cries. Gut-wrenching sobs tear through his body, and the tears I'm fighting to hold back spill out. I turn my head to look over at Mac and see that his face is wet with tears, too. He meets my eyes and nods then turns and slips out of the room.

I hold onto Jay tightly, whispering for him to let it all out.

He needs this.

He needs *me.*

Chapter Thirty-Seven

Jay

I wake to the sunlight streaming in through my window, reflecting off the golden hair splayed across my chest.

It wasn't a dream. She's really here.

Kate.

I breathe in her scent, strawberries and cream. It's so warm and familiar. I can't believe she came to me...she came *for* me. I'll have to thank Mac. It had to have been him who called her; they walked in together after all.

However, not even the distraction of my girl can calm the aching emptiness in my chest.

Sean.

I can't believe he's gone. It's so fucked up. That truck…its headlights…Sean's eyes…he knew what was going to happen. Not even an hour earlier, we'd been smiling and laughing as we talked about him becoming a dad. The horror and fear in his eyes…it's an image that is going to remain ingrained in my mind forever.

Kate stirs, and I tighten my grip around her with my good arm. I don't know how long she's staying for, but I'm not ready to let her go yet. Maybe not ever. I will grovel and beg, but I will never leave her again.

"Hey, handsome," she says, her voice husky with sleep. She tilts her head back so she's looking into my eyes. "Did you sleep?"

"A little bit," I tell her, giving her a small smile. The fact that I got any sleep at all is a miracle in itself. Every time I close my eyes I see those damn headlights…Sean's eyes. It must be her…her presence…it soothes me.

She smiles. "Mac was really worried about you."

"He called you?"

She nods against my chest. "He did. I'm glad he did. I'm glad I'm here with you."

"I'm glad you're here, too," I say, kissing her forehead. "I'm sorry for the things I said to you. I realize now that I should have let you make those decisions for yourself. You're the smartest, most beautiful person I know—

inside and out—and you would have made the right choice for yourself. I should have trusted that. I think part of me was scared that maybe you'd leave me first."

Kate lifts herself up on her elbow and looks into my eyes. "I'm not going to leave you, Jay. I can't say that we'll be together forever because shit happens, but I can say that I *want* to be together forever. I want to be with you forever. I don't ever want to leave you. I love you."

I don't waste another minute and, using my good arm, I grip the back of her head and pull her lips to mine. God, I've missed this. I've missed her. Her smell, her taste, everything. I'm about ready to tell her to take off her clothes when there's a knock at the door. I leave her with one last kiss and call out for whoever it is to come in.

Mac pokes his head in the door, smiling when he sees the two of us lying together. "I brought breakfast. Better than that hospital crap," he says, setting a brown paper bag on the table beside my bed. "I'm going to head over to see Julia."

Just like that, the heavy weight is back on my chest. I nod in acknowledgement, and he slips out of the room as quickly as he'd entered.

"Who's Julia?" Kate asks.

"Sean's wife," I tell her. It hurts to even say his name.

"Do you want to talk about it? About anything?"

I don't. I just want the hurt to stop, but I realize that in order to do that, I need to talk about it. And Kate is the only one I want to talk to.

"I just can't believe he's gone. We went to grab a bite to eat after work. I'd been acting like a real shit, missing you and feeling like an asshole. He called me out on it and made me meet him at Harry's. We had dinner and talked. He told me I didn't give you enough credit. That you were strong enough to make decisions for yourself. I was going to call you when I got home. I was gonna try to get you back. We were only a few blocks from the turnoff to his house when it happened."

I squeeze my eyes shut, then open them back up because I can't stand to see those images flashing through my mind. I've seen the scene a thousand times, but I feel like if I speak it, it'll be even more real. But seriously, what's more real than the death of your best friend? Not talking about it isn't going to bring him back.

"You don't have to talk about it. I know it's got to be hard."

"He was going to be a dad. They just found out Julia's pregnant."

Kate gasps. "Oh, my God. I can't even imagine what she must be going through."

"Me either." This went from being the happiest time of her life to the worst. All in a matter of days.

"So were you and Mac and Sean all close?"

I sigh. "Sort of. Mac and Sean were best friends all through school. They're the same age. I would tag along here and there, but being six years younger, it didn't always fly. When I moved in with Mac after my parents went to jail, they let me hang around a little bit more, and Sean and I became friends. Then when Mac arrested me, and I wouldn't speak to him, Sean was our in-between. He'd come and visit and report back to Mac. I guess we sort of bonded then and remained close ever since. Kind of crazy, huh? Two of the closest relationships in my life were built while I was in jail."

"It's not crazy at all. People are sent to us when we need them the most."

I ponder that thought and realize that it's the truth. When I'd been in prison, it was the darkest time of my life. The two brightest spots were Kate and Sean—for two very different reasons of course.

"Thanks, Sunshine," I say, kissing the top of her head.

"You're welcome, handsome."

***

I look around at the crowd of people gathered to celebrate the life of Sean Patrick Reilly. There's me, Mac, and Kate, the guys from Sean's shop, Julia and her parents and sisters, and some extended family as well.

The cemetery is also crowded with Sean's bike brothers...some are customers, others are people he's cruised with. And then there are all the other bikers. Riders from here, there, and everywhere who had heard about a fallen brother and came out to show their support and unity. The sound of all the bikes as they'd approached had been both deafening and beautiful.

It's a sendoff that Sean would be proud of. He wouldn't have wanted it any other way.

The service itself is short and sweet. In his will, Sean had specified he didn't want a long and drawn out affair. As his coffin is lowered, Julia finally breaks down. Heart-wrenching sobs come from Sean's widow, bringing tears to the eyes of the mourners. Mac waves off my offer of help and walks Julia to the waiting limo.

Kate squeezes my hand, tucking herself into my side as a tear falls down my cheek. I look down at Sean's final resting place and say goodbye to my other brother.

"I wish I'd had the chance to meet him," Kate whispers as we walk away.

"Me, too, Sunshine. Me, too."

Chapter Thirty-Eight

Kate

"Hello, Cedric," I say to my parents' butler as I walk into their home for the first time in three years. Cedric has been with my family as long as I can remember. He must be in his seventies now, and his white hair is a sharp contrast to his black suit.

"Miss Katherine," Cedric says with a warm smile and wide eyes, clearly surprised to see me. I'd always liked "the help," much to my parents' dismay—hell, I was practically raised by them. Cedric's greeting ends there as you never know when someone may be watching in my parents' home.

"Are my parents here?" I ask him, resisting the urge to hug him. His smile shows more emotion than I've seen from my mother or father in years. Aside from Casey and Jay, I'd forgotten what it was like for someone to be happy to see me.

Cedric nods. "They're having breakfast in the breakfast nook."

"Thank you, Cedric." I roll my eyes internally. Yes...my parents are *those* people. The ones who eat breakfast at one table and dinner at another. They typically have lunch out or in the sunroom. As if having three meals at one table would bring them down to the level of a commoner.

"It's wonderful to see you again, Miss." I give him one last smile as I make my way through the house towards the dining rooms.

I'm mildly surprised to see the house seems exactly as it had been when I'd left for college. You'd think my mother would have found something dated that had needed replacing, but from what I can see, everything is the same. It still looks like a museum. I smirk as I run my fingertip along the bright, white walls. Then I quickly remove my finger and feel guilty as one of the maids will likely be held responsible for any smudges I leave behind.

The breakfast nook comes into view, and I see my father seated at one end of the six-seater table and my mother at the other. They aren't speaking, or even looking at each other. My father has his nose in the paper, and my mother is tapping away on her smart phone. They haven't even noticed my arrival.

I clear my throat, and they both look up, annoyed at the interruption. I catch very brief looks of surprise on each of their faces before they school them back to cool indifference.

"Katherine," my father says. "I didn't expect to see you here."

"Why aren't you at school?" my mother adds.

"Summer vacation," I tell them, which isn't entirely a lie. I'd never taken a break for the summer though; I always took summer courses. I walk over to the table and pull out a chair, intending to sit down, but then I change my mind. I need to do this standing up. I can't give them the upper hand by being able to look down on me as they berate me for my choices.

My mother laughs. "Summer vacation? We don't pay for you to take vacations, Katherine. What are you doing here?"

If I hadn't been used to her coldness, her words might hurt, but the unconditional love I've received from my friends has shown me that I'm better than this. I'm better than the way my parents treat me. I don't deserve it.

I take a deep, calming breath, and then I let it all out. "I'm here to talk to you. To both of you," I say, looking first at my mother then my father. My mother looks amused while my father just looks bored.

Why have I been trying so hard all my life to impress these people? They couldn't care less about me. They don't care about anything.

"So talk. We don't have all day."

I wonder if my mother has a heart at all?

"I'm leaving Stanford."

"Like hell you are," my father says, slamming his hand on the table, suddenly paying attention.

If I hadn't been expecting the reaction, I'd be startled...but I was, so I'm not. I lock eyes with my father and tell him, "Yes, I am. I've already withdrawn from classes and given notice to the university."

"Well, then you'll re-enroll. I'll call the dean right now," my mother says, picking up her Blackberry.

"No!" My mother looks up at me, and I can't tell if she's surprised I've raised my voice at her or if it's the Botox. "I'm not continuing my studies at Stanford. I want to teach. I'm enrolling in a teaching program."

"That's ridiculous. You are not enrolling in a teaching program. You're going to med school. We already discussed this. It's final."

I look at my father and shake my head. "I'm not. I'm not going to med school. I wanted to want that—for you, I really did. All I've wanted my entire life was to make you proud." I look to my mother, "Both of you. But I can't do it at the expense of my own happiness anymore. I've tried to talk to you about this, and you always belittle it. I don't know what else I can do to make you understand that I'm not happy with pre-med."

"It's work, Katherine," my father says. "Work doesn't always make you happy. That's why it's called *work*."

"But it can. It can make me happy. Don't you want that for me? Don't you want me to do something that makes me happy?" I look him straight in the eyes and plead with him to understand. I plead with him to see how miserable his daughter is and for him to want her to be happy. I get nothing in response.

"This is ridiculous. I don't have time for this nonsense," my mother says, rising from her chair and moving to leave the room.

"I'm not asking for your approval," I tell them both firmly. "I'm doing this."

My mother stops walking and turns to look at me. To the people of the court, her cold eyes, the sharp lines of her face, and her beige power suit may be intimidating...but me? I'm just over it. I'm over it all.

"Well, if you think we're paying for you to just throw away your future, you've got another thing coming."

"That's right," my father agrees with her.

"I don't expect that at all. I've saved quite a bit working the past few years in California. I have enough to get myself settled in a new place. I'll take out loans for college," I say, shrugging my shoulders.

My father laughs as if this is all just a joke, as if my plans for my future are funny. Pretty soon my mother is joining him.

"You'll never last a day in the real world," my mother says. "You'll come crawling back in no time, Katherine. Mark my words. You have no idea what it's like to have real expenses. Everything has always been handed to you. You'll miss the luxuries, and you'll be back, just begging to return to Stanford. The pennies you saved from your 'job' won't get you far," she says, using air quotes around the word *job*.

"I have more than $50,000 saved from my 'job.'" I tell her.

They both sober up and, suddenly, my situation isn't so funny anymore.

"This has to do with that *criminal*, doesn't it?" my mother asks scathingly, and it takes everything I have to keep my cool. I hate that she feels the need to bring Jay into this and that she calls him a criminal. She doesn't know a thing about him.

"This has nothing to do with *Jay*. It has to do with me and what I want to do with the rest of my life. It's about my passion."

"You're making a mistake," my father says.

"Maybe I am. But it's my mistake to make." I shake my head. I'm not really sure why I came here this morning. I guess it was a last ditch effort to see if they cared about me beyond appearances. It's obvious they don't. "That's all I came to say. I'll be out of the apartment in California before the end of the month." I give them each one last look, wondering if they'll say anything...anything at all. I'm met with silence, so I turn and walk out of the room.

I hear the click of my mother's heels as she follows behind me. "And just where do you think you'll go?"

"Don't worry about me," I call over my shoulder. "I'll be just fine." Like I'll tell her where I'm going so she can have some goon watch me like she obviously did in California. No way.

"Katherine, don't you walk away from me when I'm speaking to you."

I stop and turn to face her. "What? What else do you have to say? Do you want to continue to demean my choices? You want to talk badly about the man I'm in love with? Because, yes, I'm in love with him," I tell her shocked face. "I'm finished, Mother. I've tried to talk to you and help you to understand *me*, but you won't listen. Now I'm leaving."

"If you walk out that door, don't bother coming back."

I feel the threat of tears behind my eyes at her declaration. I always knew what my parents were like, and I'd honestly expected this reaction...this possibility, but it still hurts that the only family I have would rather disown me than accept that I want something different for my life than what they want for me.

"Goodbye, Mother."

I leave my mother staring wide-eyed at my retreating form as I head for the front door. I don't hear her footsteps following, nor those of my father. When I reach the front door, Cedric is there to open it for me.

"Good luck, Bambi," he says quietly, and I tear up at the endearment I haven't heard since before I left for college.

Breaking all the "house rules," I lean in and give Cedric a hug, wrapping my arms tightly around his slender frame. He's shocked at the affection, but only for a moment before he places his arms around me. After a tender moment, I release him and step back.

"Where I'm going, Cedric, I don't need luck. But thank you, Cedric. Thank you for everything." He winks at me, and I smile. I'll miss him.

I step out into the humid, summer air and take a deep, cleansing breath.

Today is the first day of the rest of my life.

Chapter Thirty-Nine

Jay

"Whatcha doing there?"

Kate's voice startles me, and I drop the wrench from my hand. "Where the hell did you come from?" I ask, rising from my seated position beside my bike and kissing her.

That never gets old.

"I was at my parents' house," she says, kicking a rock on the gravel driveway.

"I know that. How'd you get here?" I ask, looking around. "I didn't hear your car?"

She looks down at her feet, and I lift her chin with my greasy fingers. If she wasn't so distracted, she would have given me hell for that. Her big brown eyes look into mine, and she looks nervous...scared even.

"What's going on, Sunshine?"

She takes a deep breath, then lets it out. "The conversation with them went about as well as to be expected. They think I'm crazy. I'm sure they're disappointed. They told me...my mother said if I left I shouldn't bother coming back." She shrugs her shoulders and smiles a little. "I left the car in the driveway. I don't want anything to remind me of their disapproval. I took a cab."

I wrap my good arm around her shoulder and pull her into my chest. "I'm sorry they're assholes. But I'm proud of you."

I hear her sniffle, and for a moment, I think she's crying. That is until she wiggles free and scrunches up her nose. She points her finger at me, "You stink! And you're dirty." She looks down at her white t-shirt and sure enough there are a few black and grey smudges from where she was pressed against me.

"You love me anyway," I say, giving her a smile.

"Yeah...I do." She takes a few small steps forward and leans into my chest. I put my arm around her again, careful not to club her with my cast. This...this right here is the stuff dreams are made of. I feel like I can be anything...do anything...as long as this girl is by my side.

A week ago, I was a mess. I'd been lying in a hospital bed feeling like my life was over. My best friend was gone. My girl was across the country. And, somehow, I was alive. Alive and alone. There were more than a few moments where I'd wished I could press the little red button long enough for a lethal dose of painkillers to come out...figures they'd moderate that shit. But it's good that they do, because if I had offed myself...I wouldn't have this right here.

"You okay?" I ask her, knowing it's a silly question. If anyone is okay under duress, it's Kate. She's the most resilient person I know.

"Mm hmm."

She pulls away, and I feel the loss. I'm complete mush as far as she's concerned...if Sean could see me now, he'd probably be razzing me for it. Hell, he probably can see me now and is getting a good laugh at my expense. Or he's up there smiling and thinking, "It's about damn time."

"I'm gonna need a new car," Kate says. "Not a *new* car, but a new-to-me car."

I nod in agreement. "Let me put these tools away and then I'll ask Mac if we can take his truck."

Not only can I not ride my bike with my broken arm, but it also has some damage from the wreck. Most of it is surface stuff—scratches and dents—but a few parts need to be replaced. It's probably good that I can't ride it right now...gives me time to fix it.

Kate works beside me, helping me set the tools in my toolbox, and when we're done, she carries the toolbox while I roll my bike into the garage. Then I take her hand in my good one, and we walk into the house.

While I'd been in prison, Mac had graduated from that rickety two bedroom apartment to a small, three bedroom ranch house in a nicer part of town. It's plenty big enough for him, and he's happy to have me and Kate here with him until we figure out our next move.

Things are...different between Mac and me now. Better, for sure. Sean's death—though it's only been a few days—has brought us closer together. Sean was Mac's friend, too, and his death crushed him as much as it did me. I'd been so busy wallowing in my own self-pity that I hadn't thought about that. We both felt like we lost a brother, but at least we still had each other.

When Kate and I enter the kitchen, Mac looks up from the paper. He smiles when he sees us hand-in-hand. "What are you two up to?" he asks.

"Jay's gonna take me to get a new-to-me car," Kate smiles back. She and Mac get along great. He gives her complete credit for pulling me out of my funk. I'm not sure where I'd be if he hadn't called her, and she hadn't come.

"What happened to your car?" he asks, sitting up straight.

I lean against the counter while Kate sits at the table, in the seat across from Mac. She picks up one of the muffins she'd baked this morning. "I left it at my parents' house. Out with the old…new beginning…all that."

While she's picking at her muffin, Mac looks up at me and raises his eyebrow. I know he's silently asking me if she's okay. I give him a quick nod, and he relaxes back in his seat.

"Can we take your truck? We won't be gone too long."

"Take as long as you need. I don't have any place to be until my shift starts, and I'll be taking the cruiser anyway."

I look over to Kate who is still picking at her muffin. "When do you want to go, babe?"

Kate looks up and smiles, a genuine smile. "Whenever you're ready." See? My girl is resilient.

"Let me go wash up, and I'll be right down. You might want to change your shirt," I laugh, pointing to her new stains.

Suddenly remembering the grease, she looks down at her shirt and scowls. "Dammit, Jason!"

"Ohh damn, she just full-named you. Better watch out," Mac laughs, then quickly straightens up when Kate glares at him. "You shouldn't get grease on your girlfriend's clothes," he then says to me in his cop voice, earning a smirk from Kate.

"Kiss ass," I mutter as I leave the room. I hear the two of them joking around and laughing together as I make my way to my bedroom, and the sound makes me smile.

I know we won't stay here forever, but it sure is nice having the people I care about most all under one roof.

***

The following morning, Mac, Kate, and I pile into her newish Honda Civic and drive downtown to the office of the attorney handling Sean's estate. Today is the reading of the will, and Julia has asked us to be present. I would have rather gone anywhere but there, but as Mac reminded me, we need to be supportive of Julia for Sean. That's what Sean would have wanted. And damn if he hadn't been right.

"We're all here to read the will of Sean Reilly," the attorney, Warren Perry, says as he takes a seat at the head of the table. His assistant—or whoever she is—walks around the table handing out thick packets of paper to Julia, Mac, and me. Sean's parents are long gone, and he didn't have any siblings, so it's just us three who had been closest to him.

Kate's hand is resting on my thigh under the table, and she squeezes her support as the lawyer drones on about legal stuff I barely understand. Then he says my name and Kate squeezes harder.

"In the matter of his business, Reilly's Bikes, Mr. Reilly leaves proprietorship to his wife, Julia McKinley Reilly, and to Mac Charles Spencer and Jason Frances Spencer."

"Excuse me?" I hear Mac say.

"Frances?" Kate whispers.

"Ownership will be split in the following way," Perry continues, as if Mac hadn't spoken. "Fifty-two percent to Mrs. Reilly, and twenty-four percent each, to Mac and Jason Spencer."

"Did you know about this?" Mac asks Julia.

"I suspected it when Mr. Perry asked me to have you both be here today," Julia says quietly. She's holding herself together quite well, but I can tell she wants to bolt as badly as I do.

"Are you okay with this?" Mac asks, more softly this time.

Julia gives him a small smile. "Of course. It's what Sean wanted. I can't run that shop by myself anyway. I don't know a thing about motorcycles." Her voice breaks on that last word, a painful reminder of how we'd lost Sean. I'm not sure Julia could stand to look at a motorcycle, let alone run a motorcycle shop.

"We'll take care of it," I assure her, and she nods her appreciation.

"Thank you. Sean really loved the two of you." Julie sniffles and a tear spills from her right eye, and damn if it doesn't make me want to cry, too.

What was Sean thinking leaving his business to me? Even just part of it. I don't know how to run a business. I look to Kate who is quietly sitting beside me. What does this mean for us? If I'm part owner of Reilly's Bikes, that means I have to be here...in Columbia...to run the shop. What if she wants to go back to California? What if she wants to go to school somewhere else?

What if I lose her again?

Chapter Forty

Kate

Jay has been distant since the reading of the will. He keeps telling me nothing is wrong, but I call bullshit. He's not that difficult to read. I know he's panicking because suddenly he's tied to a life in Columbia and just days before our possibilities were endless. We could have thrown a dart at a map and made that place our home. I know he's afraid I won't want to stay in South Carolina, that I'll find someplace else where I want to go to school and leave him behind.

The silly man shouldn't worry so much.

What he doesn't know is that back when he and I first talked about my dream of becoming a teacher, I'd applied to transfer to a few different schools...some in California and some in South Carolina.

And I got in.

To the University of South Carolina.

In Columbia.

Casey called me as soon as the acceptance package arrived. Yeah...I might be a little evil for keeping it from Jay, but I want to surprise him. I can't wait to surprise him.

Right now, I'm back in California. Jay thinks I'm here visiting Casey and Decker, which I am, but he has no idea I'm also moving out of my apartment. The lease is in my parents' name and since that connection has been severed, it's time to leave here. Plus, Casey and Decker rented a new place between Stanford and the University of San Francisco, where they'll both be finishing out their senior years.

But Jay doesn't know all that, either.

"I can't believe we're not going to live together anymore," Casey whines as I take the last book off my bookshelf and neatly place it in a box. "And I can't believe you're moving across the country."

I roll my eyes. "You and Decker are both *from* across the country. You'll be returning to South Carolina after graduation."

"Yeah, but that's like a whole year away."

"We'll still visit," I tell her, taping the box shut.

"Yeah…I guess. But I'll still miss you, roomie."

I set the packing tape down and take my roommate/best friend in a hug, being careful not to squeeze her too tight. "I'll miss you, too."

"It's like the end of an era," Casey laments.

"Oh, dear lord," I mutter under my breath. She's acting like this is a permanent separation. We'll be living in the same state again very soon. "Don't you have to finish packing?"

"Yeah, I better make sure Decker's putting everything where I told him to."

I laugh, she sure has him wrapped around her finger. I'm so happy for them both. Casey shines when she's around Decker, and Decker looks at her like she walks on water. They're a match made in heaven, for sure.

"My flight is at ten o'clock," I remind her, and she frowns again.

"I know."

"You sure you and Decker are okay with shipping my stuff for me? I already wrote Mac's address on all the boxes."

"Yeah, it's fine." She shrugs. "Decker met a couple guys at the gym who said they'd help with the heavy lifting."

"There are only like five boxes," I tell her.

"And three of those are books," she deadpans.

She's keeping most of the furniture and household items, the rest of the stuff we're donating. I sure don't need or want any of it for my new life with Jay. All I'm bringing with me are my books, some DVDs, my clothes, photos, and some trinkets.

New life...here I come!

***

You know those chick flicks where the man is at the airport, waiting patiently for the woman at the escalator? Then they see each other, they smile wide and maybe shed a few tears before throwing themselves into each other's arms?

Do you know what I'm talking about?

Can you picture it?

That *so* wasn't what mine and Jay's reunion looked like.

I disembark the plane and run—I mean I run like someone is chasing me—through the concourse with one destination—one person—in mind.

Jay.

I miss him something fierce. I'd only been in California for five days, but it was enough.

Heck, ten minutes is enough when you're separated from the love of your life.

I run by the security check in, garnering a few interested glances from TSA, all the way to where people are waiting for their loved ones. I stop. I look left, then right. No Jay.

Where the hell is he?

"Sunshine!"

My frown turns into a megawatt grin as I turn towards the voice. There he is. All six feet of him, looking gorgeous as ever with his tattooed arms and smiling gray eyes.

I drop my carry-on and run—full-force—into his waiting arms. Only he doesn't have two functioning arms, he has one, so he can't quite catch me when I jump on him, and we land with a thud on the floor. The people around us gasp and look on with shocked expressions.

"I'm so sorry," I tell him, thankful his head didn't smack the tile floor.

He just smiles up at me. "I'm not," he says, before taking my mouth in a bruising kiss that is not at all suitable for public viewing.

"Ahem," a throat clears somewhere above us. I look up to see an airport security officer glowering down at us.

"Sorry," I say, climbing off Jay and getting to my feet. I reach out my hand and help him up, then scurry off to collect my bag and leave Jay to deal with the angry officer.

It's okay; my surprise will more than make up for it.

***

"I missed you so much," I tell Jay, trailing kisses across his naked chest.

"I missed you, too."

I'm in my favorite place, curled up beside him on his bed, his good arm wrapped around me, and my body deliciously sore from three rounds of lovemaking. Thank God Mac is at work; he would have arrested us for disturbing the peace.

"I couldn't wait to get back home to you."

"Home, huh?" he asks.

"Home," I confirm. "I have something I need to talk to you about."

I hear his breath catch and feel his body tense against me. He's still afraid I'm going to leave him.

"What's up?" he says, attempting to sound casual.

"A while back...I applied to some colleges...education programs, you know?"

He nods stiffly. "And?"

"I got in to my first choice."

I see his Adam's apple move as he swallows. "What was your first choice?"

"USC," I tell him, purposely not clarifying whether I mean University of South Carolina or University of Southern California. Yeah...I'm definitely a little bit evil.

"USC?" he asks.

I nod and wait. And wait. He doesn't say a word.

"Jay? Say something."

He rolls over so he's hovering over me, holding himself up with his good hand. "You'd better mean University of South Carolina or you're going to be in big trouble," he says in his most menacing voice. It's quite adorable.

I keep a straight face as long as I can, until I can't contain it any longer. I smile. He smiles—the brightest smile I've ever seen on his face. Then he kisses me...hard.

"You are in so much trouble," he says as he kisses down my neck.

"Why?" I gasp as his tongue grazes my breast, touching everywhere but where I want it to...where I need it to.

"Tormenting me like that...I'll show you torment."

"Jay," I laugh as he licks and nips my neck, down my chest, my breasts, and my side...straight down to my core. I squirm beneath him, urging him to go where I so desperately need him.

"You want me to stop?" he teases.

"No! Please don't stop."

He doesn't stop. He keeps going, and going, and going.

And let me tell you…round four beat out rounds one, two, and three combined.

Epilogue

Kate

Five months later...

"I now pronounce you husband and wife. You may kiss your bride."

The guests cheer as Casey and Decker kiss. Bird seed is thrown in the air and bubbles are blown as they make their way down the dock—their dock—and into the large backyard of Casey's mother's house, which has been transformed into a winter wonderland.

There's a huge party tent—complete with heaters—decorated to the max to represent Casey and Decker's winter wedding. Well...as winter as a wedding can get in South Carolina seeing as today's low is fifty degrees, despite it being December. White lights hang from the ceiling, bathing everything in a soft, romantic glow. Decorations in white and silver tastefully adorn the tables.

As Casey's only bridesmaid, and maid of honor by default, I'm dressed in a floor-length silver gown with crystal beading around the neckline. Casey is wearing a gorgeous white, strapless ball gown with crystals sewn into the fabric. She looks like a princess. She's beautiful. Decker and his dad, who is also his best man, are both wearing black tuxes with black shirts, only Decker's tie and vest are white to match Casey's dress, and Mr. Abrams's are silver to match mine.

The wedding was beautiful, and who cares if the bride and groom were already married by a Justice of the Peace a couple months ago? I dare anyone to challenge Casey and Decker. They deserve happiness more than anyone I know. Except maybe Jay and me; we deserve lots of happiness, too.

There hadn't been a dry eye in the house—err, yard—when Casey walked down to the dock to meet Decker, escorted by her mom and Decker's parents. Casey was surely missing her dad today, but we all knew he was looking down on her for this very special moment. And, while she would have loved having her dad walk her down the aisle, the next best people where there in his place. He wouldn't have wanted it any other way, except to be there himself, of course.

It's been a busy few months since I left California. I've just finished my first semester at the University of South Carolina, and I couldn't be happier. I love it. The education program is amazing and just what my soul needed—aside from Jay. Jay is doing great running Sean's shop. It was a little rough for him at first; Sean left behind some pretty big shoes to fill. But with Mac and Julia's help, Jay got a handle on things.

I haven't heard a word from my parents since I'd walked out of their house, and I'm not at all surprised. I thought I'd feel some kind of void, but I don't. I have a new family now with Jay and Mac, and even Julia. I've spent a lot of time with her over the past few months, even attending some of her doctor's appointments with her. She's due to have her baby boy in February and wants to name him Sean Patrick after his daddy.

And, of course, I have Casey and Decker and their parents. I haven't been able to visit Mrs. Evans as much as I'd like with school, but now that I'm on winter break and Casey and Decker are too, I plan to spend as much time in Charleston as I can.

I smile as Jay slides his hand into mine. "You look beautiful," he whispers in my ear.

"Shh," I tell him. "The bride is the only one you're supposed to tell she looks beautiful."

"She does," he agrees, "but so do you."

I lean against him, and we sway together as we watch Casey and Decker dance to their first dance, "Red on a Rose" by Alan Jackson.

"Think we'll be as happy as they are some day?" I ask him.

"We already are, Sunshine. We already are."

"I'm so happy my car broke down that day," I say, looking into his eyes. He dips his head down and gives me a quick, but sensuous, kiss.

"And I'm so happy I was finally in the right place at the right time."

Acknowledgements

I'd like to thank my family—my husband, parents, sisters, brothers, nieces, nephews, etc.—for their support during this very random journey of mine. You've all been wonderful and I appreciate that. An enormous thank you to the readers who keep reading my stuff. You're all amazing. My beta readers, proofreader, and editor—you all rock! Thank you for helping me to make this book what it is today. Thank you to my reader group, Jennifer's Chapter Chicks, for being my sounding board, whether it's about something specific or something totally random, you ladies know how to help a girl out! Thank you to Natasha at Read Review Repeat for organizing all the blog activities. Your patience with my nonsense is astounding. Thank you Cassy at Pink Ink Designs for the cover, amazing work as always. Thank you to all the bloggers who have helped spread the word about the cover reveal and the release. I wouldn't have a single reader without you all.

About the Author

Jennifer lives in South Carolina with her husband and their three fur-kids. She is in grad school, pursuing a Masters in Psychology for Clinical Counseling. When she is not at work or taking classes, she is either reading or writing. Books have always been a passion. She also enjoys spending time with her family, traveling to new places, and music.

Connect With Me

Email: jenniferlallenauthor@gmail.com

Website: www.jenniferlallenauthor.com

Facebook: www.facebook.com/jallenauthor

Twitter: https://twitter.com/AuthorJenniferA

Also by Jennifer L. Allen

Our Moon (JACT 1)
Hearts in the Sand (JACT 2)

Change of Heart (Second Chances 1)

www.ingramcontent.com/pod-product-compliance
Lightning Source LLC
La Vergne TN
LVHW091024080826
845145LV00002B/344

* 9 7 8 0 9 9 6 4 5 6 5 7 9 *